Samuel French Acting Edition

Wonderland Wives

by Buddy Thomas

Conceived by Phil Poluliah &
Buddy Thomas

I0591719

ılı SAMUEL FRENCH ılı

SAMUELFRENCH.COM   SAMUELFRENCH.CO.UK

FOR PRODUCTION ENQUIRIES

UNITED STATES AND CANADA
Info@SamuelFrench.com
1-866-598-8449

UNITED KINGDOM AND EUROPE
Plays@SamuelFrench.co.uk
020-7255-4302

Each title is subject to availability from Samuel French, depending upon country of performance. Please be aware that *WONDERLAND WIVES* may not be licensed by Samuel French in your territory. Professional and amateur producers should contact the nearest Samuel French office or licensing partner to verify availability.

MUSIC USE NOTE

Licensees are solely responsible for obtaining formal written permission from copyright owners to use copyrighted music in the performance of this play and are strongly cautioned to do so. If no such permission is obtained by the licensee, then the licensee must use only original music that the licensee owns and controls. Licensees are solely responsible and liable for all music clearances and shall indemnify the copyright owners of the play(s) and their licensing agent, Samuel French, against any costs, expenses, losses and liabilities arising from the use of music by licensees. Please contact the appropriate music licensing authority in your territory for the rights to any incidental music.

IMPORTANT BILLING AND CREDIT REQUIREMENTS

If you have obtained performance rights to this title, please refer to your licensing agreement for important billing and credit requirements.

WONDERLAND WIVES was first produced by the Nearly Naked Theatre, Damon Dering, Artistic Director, in April 2016. The production was directed by Damon Dering, with scenic design by Kenneth Anthony, scenic artistry by Paul Wilson, lighting design by Clare Burnett, sound design by Patti Swartz, costume design by Douglas Loynd, props design by Jay Templeton and Ralph Roberts, and hair & makeup design by Terre Steed. The production stage manager was Joanne Gregg. The cast was as follows:

ACTOR 1 – SNOW . . . . Nathalie Cadieux

ACTOR 2 – BELLE . . . . Bill Dyer

ACTOR 3 – CINDY . . . . Matthew R. Harris

ACTOR 4 – ROSE . . . . Laura Anne Kenney

ACTOR 5 – BRUCE/BEAST AND CHARMING . . . . .David Nelson

ACTOR 6 – FAIRY GODMOTHER; ALICE;
       MAGIC MIRROR; QUEEN . . . . Terre Steed

CHARACTERS

Wonderland Wives is designed to be performed by a cast of six actors as follows:

Actor 1 – **SNOW**

Actor 2 – **BELLE**

Actor 3 – **CINDY**

Actor 4 – **ROSE**

Actor 5 – **BRUCE/BEAST** & **CHARMING**

Actor 6 – **FAIRY GODMOTHER; ALICE; MAGIC MIRROR; QUEEN**

SETTING

The action of the play takes place in a magical kingdom, long ago, and far away.

AUTHOR'S NOTES

Wonderland Wives is a fractured fairy tale with strong language and adult situations, and is meant for mature audiences with very immature taste. The world premiere production used cross gender casting for the roles of Belle, Cindy, Fairy Godmother, Alice, and the Queen, and that is encouraged but not required. In other words, some or all roles may be played by men in drag.

ACT ONE

Scene One

*(Lights rise on **FAIRY GODMOTHER**.)*

(She lounges on a comfortable pool chair. Her back is to the audience, for now.)

(Beside her sits a large tropical drink with an umbrella in it, which she will sip from, from time to time. Several empty glasses of the same kind sit nearby. She's been knocking them back. She speaks on a phone, mid-conversation, as lights rise.)

FAIRY GODMOTHER. Honey, I just can't do it, I told you, I am in the middle of the South Pacific, I would never make it in time... No, no, we've been through this, I don't travel that way any more. I am a six hundred and fifty year old woman and I have officially retired that damned bubble. Do you know what that thing does to your back?

> *(She turns around and we see for the first time that she is in her traditional "fairy godmother" garb, but with several leis around her neck.)*

Oh, for the love of God, Cindy, if you start crying again... I do not know when you became so needy. I think all those years you spent as a maid warped your fragile mind...Well it's not as if you didn't know I was hanging up that wand... Cindy, you stop that. Of course I still care, but can't I just have one moment of peace without this phone ringing off the hook day after day after day with all your endless marital woes?! First you find out Mr. Wonderful is frigid in the sack, and then you catch him in bed with that mermaid. And who knew he was connected to the mob? Now he's in jail for sex trafficking, tax evasion, and racketeering, and you *still* plan on taking him back? You do what you want, honey, but if this leads to more of your hysterical calls at every hour of the night, I'm changing this number for good… I know… I know… Now listen, honey, I have to go. There's a six-foot-four Polynesian on the other side of the pool and from what I can tell, he's got quite a wand of his own… Bye now Cindy. Enjoy the party. I mailed you a bunt cake…but Cindy…take it easy on the portions. Snow says you've put on a few pounds.

(Blackout.)

Scene Two

(Lights up on the drawing room of Snow White's castle.)

*(**BELLE** and **SNOW** are setting up for a party. They will be setting out food and drink, hanging streamers, etc. throughout the scene.)*

BELLE. Snow, honey, it sure is big of ya to hold Cindy's party here. All those little monsters running around my pad, we'd never have a lick of fun.

SNOW. Oh, Belle. Don't talk about your children so. They're angels.

BELLE. They're animals. Of course that's why you like 'em. If someone's got a paw or a beak, you just start singing.

SNOW. It's my way, I suppose.

BELLE. Well, I don't know how you do it. All you've been through and you've never changed.

SNOW. Always use your royal night cream.

BELLE. Not your looks, honey, your attitude. Considering your whole life is in shambles –

SNOW. Now, now, let's not talk about me. Today's for Cindy. She's welcoming back her wonderful prince, and we all need to be here to celebrate their blessed reunion.

BELLE. Well, he's been in the slammer the past ten years, so I don't know how much he'll be celebrating once he lays his eyes on her.

SNOW. Now Belle, you stop all this. You of all people should appreciate inner beauty.

BELLE. Yeah? Try living in my place for a day and we'll see how you feel about inner beauty. That out of work tub of lard lazing all over my castle guzzling beer and belching up, it's enough to make me wish I married that candlestick instead.

SNOW. Oh, Belle, you know you don't mean that. Now how does everything look?

BELLE. Real sweet, Snow, honey. I don't know about all these salads, but –

SNOW. We're trying to set a good example for Cindy.

BELLE. Oh give it up, Snow, she's passed examples. The last time that bitch ate a vegetable, she was riding around in magic pumpkins. If she swallows a carrot at this point, her colon'll go into shock and explode.

SNOW. Belle, I mean it, I won't listen to another word. Really, you don't have a kind thing to say about anyone these days.

BELLE. Well, excuse me, Miss Goody Goody. I suppose you'll be saying all sorts of kind things if we have another glass slipper incident.

SNOW. I'm sure she learned her lesson by now.

BELLE. Don't you know she's crackin' through a pair a week?

SNOW. Ohh, Belle.

BELLE. Shatterin' slippers all over the kingdom. It's disgraceful, I tell ya. Rapunzel says when she busted through the last ones, she nearly sliced off her big toe.

(A grand doorbell rings.)

SNOW. Ohh, I hope that's not the guests already.

(Sing-songy, running to the door:)

I'M COMING. JUST A MINUTE!

*(She flings open the door with a flourish. **BRUCE** a.k.a. **BEAST** stands there. He is bearded, bloated, beer-bellied, in a soiled t-shirt and ripped jeans. He holds a tall can of beer labeled "Royal Suds," and it is probably his fifth one of the day. He's a complete mess.)*

Oh! Bruce! How wonderful to see you!

BRUCE. Heya, Snow. What's cookin'?

BELLE. Jesus Christ, what the hell is that thing doing here?

(She stalks over to the door.)

Hey! You! You're supposed to be home babysitting that Goddamned brood!

BRUCE. Relax. That wood puppet with the big nose stopped by selling cookies and I asked him to sit over a while.

BELLE. What are you, crazy?! They'll use him as firewood! Don't you remember what they did to Tinker Bell?!

SNOW. At least the wing replacement surgery went well.

BELLE. I can't take it anymore! Why didn't you tell me you still had some of that beast gene in you before you knocked me up?!

BRUCE. Listen baby, how was I supposed to know?

BELLE. Baby. Baby! I *wish* I had a baby! Instead I spit out a fucking LITTER!

SNOW. Belle, please!!

BELLE. You please! You try squeezing fourteen warthogs outa *your* cooch!

BRUCE. Hey now those are my sons you're talkin' about.

BELLE. Sons?! That's a laugh. The doctor didn't know whether to put 'em in a cradle or a cage!!

SNOW. Perhaps I'll go check on the peach cobbler.

(She slinks off.)

BELLE. You still haven't said what you're doing here, you son of a bitch.

BRUCE. What, I can't welcome back my old pal, Charming?

BELLE. Your old pal's gonna love what you've turned into. Hell, between you and Cindy, he'll be surprised there's a pork chop left in the land!

BRUCE. *(Tries to hold her.)* Come on, Belle. Gimme a break. Can't we try to get along?

BELLE. Can't you try to get a job?! You lay around all day and all night, stinkin' up that castle, which is in foreclosure by the way, in case you forgot.

BRUCE. How can I forget when you never stop bitchin' about it? And there's no jobs! You damn well know that as well as I do.

BELLE. Snow told you she'd get you a job in that mine, diggin' diamonds!

BRUCE. I ain't workin' with no dwarves!

> *(**SNOW** re-enters, holding a platter. There is a little blue bird in her hair.)*

SNOW. Fresh peach cobbler!

BELLE. So now not only are you a drunk, and a pig, and a lay-about, you're also a racist?!

BRUCE. You can't talk to me like that!

BELLE. I can and I will. I want a divorce!

BRUCE. You don't mean it.

BELLE. I certainly do mean it. Snow, can I stay here with you?

SNOW. Well, I…

BELLE. Then it's settled. I'll send for my things.

BRUCE. But baby, sweetheat –

BELLE. *(Pushes him out the door.)* Blow it out your ass, you hairy gorilla. We're through!

> *(Slam. He is gone. **BELLE** collapses on the floor and bursts into tears.)*

Oh, Snow. Can you believe the way he talks to me?

SNOW. Well, I must say –

BELLE. All I ever wanted was to be a princess living happily ever after in a golden tower, and now I'm nothing but an old maid like you!

SNOW. Belle, I am no old maid, Prince John is simply lost, that's all. He'll be back any day now.

BELLE. *(Stands. Instantly hardened again.)* Sister, that man went out for a bucket of milk six years ago.

SNOW. You needn't remind me –

BELLE. Just get your head outa the clouds, Snow, and face the music. Ya been dumped.

SNOW. *(Quickly growing frazzled until she is hysterical.)* That simply isn't true, Belle, dear, I am still the fairest in the land, and John simply went out for a bucket of milk and got lost in the Frazzlefoot Forest, or the Whistling Woods or the Maddening Moor, you see, he was never good with directions, and he will be back as soon as he finds his way back, which will be any day now, you see, I'm still the fairest, THE FAIREST, YOU HEAR?!

> (**BELLE** *stares at her.*)

BELLE. *(Deadpan.)* There's a bird in your hair.

SNOW. *(Snapping out of it.)* What? A –? Huh? Oh, oh yes.

> *(She pulls the bird gently out of her hair, puts it on her finger, and trills out a few melodic bars of "la, la, la, la, la," to which the bird responds with a few chirps.)*

BELLE. Oh, Jesus.

SNOW. What's that, Bonnie Blue?

> *(More chirps.)*

A monster approaches the castle?

> *(More chirps.)*

Ohh dear! Belle, what should we do?

> (**BELLE** *has looked out the window, and rolls her eyes.*)

BELLE. Tell that bird to get spectacles.

> *(The doorbell rings, and **BELLE** swings it open. There stands **CINDY**. She looks like she swallowed the stepmother and both stepsisters. She is just enormous. She is squeezed into a beautiful gown five times too small for her, and it is bursting at the seams. Her face has probably been lifted five times too many, and the last one didn't take. She wears a face full of make-up, poorly applied. One giant lash is probably falling off. Her hair is a big bouffant mess, and a crown hangs haphazardly tilted to one side. And on her feet, glass slippers. Her feet do not*

> *even fit into them entirely, and when she walks, she*
> *will tiptoe around in huge, unsteady gaits.)*

BELLE. *(Cont.)* Cindy! Darling! Just look at you!

CINDY. *(Barreling into the room.)* Heya, Belle. It's hotter than hell out there, Snow. Ya got anything to drink?

SNOW. Oh, why yes. The royal garden honeybees just brewed a lovely pitcher of mead.

CINDY. *(Sees the bird on **SNOW**'s finger.)* Hey, lookit you, Snow. Ya went all out! Passed hors d'oeuvres, and everything!

> *(She grabs the bird off **SNOW**'s finger and shoves it*
> *into her mouth, biting it in half. Blue feathers fly*
> *everywhere.)*

SNOW. Oh my God!!

> *(She collapses in a chair, in horror.)*

CINDY. *(Spits it on the floor.)* Undercooked.

BELLE. Yes, well it's hard to find good blue bird these days.

CINDY. Ain't that the truth, what else ya got in this joint?

> *(She will rustle through the food on the table*
> *through the following.)*

SNOW. Really, Cindy, we should wait for the other guests before dining.

CINDY. Dine, shmine, it's my party, ain't it?

SNOW. Well, a welcome home banquet for your beloved –

CINDY. My beloved better be glad he's still got a home after he slept with that piece of seafood.

BELLE. Oh, Cindy let it go already.

SNOW. Belle's right, Cindy. This is your chance for everlasting happiness.

BELLE. Well don't get carried away.

CINDY. I was pickin' scales outa my bed for a month.

BELLE. Doll, just put it behind ya. No one's seen Ariel for years and years.

SNOW. I'm sure she was so embarrassed about the whole shameful incident that she swam straight back to Mermaidtopia to be with her own people.

CINDY. *(Sinister.)* She's swimmin' with the fishes, all right.

SNOW. Anyway, it's all over, and now your Prince Charming is coming home to you. Oh, Cindy, isn't this the happiest day of your life?

CINDY. *(She's now ruffled through all the food dishes.)* What's all THIS?!

SNOW. Why, that's vegetable cassoulet, Cindy. Wild mushrooms, carrots, garbonzo beans –

CINDY. GarbonWHAT? Do I look like the fucking white rabbit to you?! Where's the wild boar?! Where's the leg of lamb?! Where are the royal creamy poofs?!

SNOW. We're not having royal creamy poofs, Cindy. This is a healthy meal!

CINDY. You blithering idiot! Can't you do anything right? This is MY party and you make bean pie?

BELLE. Honey calm down, you're gonna crack those pumps again.

CINDY. *(She's gone hysterical.)* I want fried chicken! I want creamy poofs!

SNOW. Cindy!

CINDY. *(She hurls everything off the table and stomps all over it.)* Fuck you! Fuck you! I'm going to market and I'll get it all myself!

> *(She stomps out the door.)*

BELLE. *(Runs out the door after her.)* Cindy, come back!

> *(Suddenly from outside the door, we hear the loud sound of glass shattering.* **SNOW** *collapses to the floor and bursts into tears.)*

SNOW. Ohhh, what's happened to all of us? Why can't it be like it was when we were young and there was magic and we had everything our hearts desired?

> *(She gets up off the floor, and goes to a curtain on the wall. She pulls a cord, and the curtain parts to*

reveal the **MAGIC MIRROR**. **SNOW** *wipes her eyes, pulls herself together, and looks into the mirror.)*

SNOW. *(Cont.)* Mirror, mirror, that I stole from the Queen. Who is the fairest there has been?

(Smoke wisps float behind the **MAGIC MIRROR**, *and a mysterious face appears in it.)*

MAGIC MIRROR. Snow White, with skin just like a dream.

Held up with tucks…and beauty cream.

Your hair as black as raven's eye.

Colored daily with royal dye.

Extra pounds are not a hurdle

When shoved inside the tightest girdle.

So, yes, Snow White, you still are fair.

SNOW. Ohhh, Mirror, thank you!

MAGIC MIRROR. So long as I don't closely stare.

But be aware, and understand

Another comes here quite unplanned

Who is now *fairest* in the land.

SNOW. Say WHAT?!

MAGIC MIRROR. Bye now! Gotta go!

(Poof! The face disappears in a cloud of smoke.)

SNOW. You get back here right this second! Mirror! Mirror!

*(***BELLE** *re-enters.)*

BELLE. Can you believe that dame?

SNOW. *(Beside herself.)* Wha –? Huhh? What?

BELLE. She busted outa those shoes again. There's glass all over your stoop. The bitch was high tailin' it to that market so fast she almost fell in the moat… Hey whatcha got there?

*(***SNOW** *quickly tries to close the curtain on the mirror, but she's too late.)*

SNOW. Nothing, it's nothing.

BELLE. *(Goes to the mirror, pulls back the curtain.)* Nothin', my ass. You lifted that magic mirror from ol' Queenie poo.

SNOW. So what if I did? What does a dead woman need with a looking glass?

BELLE. Snow, you dirty dog you. You ain't quite as pure as the first flakes of winter after all. I'm proud of ya.

SNOW. Well, well, I don't want to talk about it. Look at this awful mess. Ohh Belle, the party is ruined.

BELLE. So. Does this thing work on anyone?

SNOW. Thing-what? No! *(She slams the curtain shut.)* Get away from it. It's mine, you hear? And no one can know about this, Belle. I mean it.

BELLE. Geez, keep your panties on, honey. What's gotten into you all of a sudden?

SNOW. N-nothing. I'm fine. Just help me clean up this mess before the rest of the guests arrive.

> *(The doorbell rings.)*

Ohhh, it's too late.

BELLE. Relax already, I'll get it. We're roomies now, remember?

> *(She flings open the door and there stands **ALICE**. Yes, that **ALICE**. She is, shall we say, a very mature adult woman now, but she still wears exactly the same outfit from her youthful adventures down the hole. The look is very Bette Davis à la Baby Jane. She has wild, googly eyes and a crazy, wide smile, and she holds a sparkly little gift box, tied with ribbon.)*

Oh. Hell. No.

SNOW. Alice!

BELLE. Who the hell invited you, you raving lunatic?!

ALICE. *(Crazy; sing-songy.)* I heard you were throwing the most perfectly marvelous tea party and I simply would not miss it for the world.

SNOW. Oh, Alice, sweetheart, this is no tea party.

ALICE. *(Marching right into the room.)* It is now, and I brought the tea!

(She opens the little box and pulls out three tea bags.)

ALICE. *(Cont.)* This one makes you smaller. And this one makes you tall. And this one makes you grow a third titty.

BELLE. Old lady, someone needs to lock you up and throw away the key.

SNOW. Belle, please.

BELLE. She's been puffin' it up with that caterpillar again. Ugh, she reeks of the stuff.

SNOW. Now Alice, I'm sorry but this is a private affair.

ALICE. Well, I'll be a good girl, I will.

SNOW. No, you don't understand. This is a celebration for Cinderella and – Prince Charming.

*(**ALICE** suddenly darkens.)*

ALICE. Prince – who?

SNOW. Yes, so you see –

ALICE. But he's…away. He was sent away.

SNOW. That's right, but he served his time, and today he returns, so –

ALICE. They let him out, after what he did to me?!

SNOW. He did many things to many people, but he's paid for his crimes and he's a changed man.

ALICE. Changed?!

SNOW. Alice, we know what happened, and that's why –

ALICE. Know what happened? Know what happened? Do you know he paid off a debt by selling me to that deck of cards?! I was locked up, ravaged. They had their way with me! Day in. Day out. All fifty-two of them! Do you know what it's like to take it in a sling from the Ten of Clubs?!

BELLE. Sounds like a party to me.

ALICE. He can't be out.

SNOW. Alice, I see this news has caught you by surprise, so –

ALICE. *(Stalking toward the door; Darkly.)* Surprise. I'll give him a surprise. Ohh, I've got a simply marvelous surprise in store for him.

BELLE. That's great, honey. Now could I get the number for that Ten of Clubs?

> *(**ALICE** exits.)*

SNOW. Ohh dear. What does she mean? Alice, come back!

> *(**SNOW** runs out after her, leaving **BELLE** alone. **BELLE** looks after them for a moment to make sure they are gone, and then she slinks over to the curtained **MIRROR**. She takes another quick peek to make sure **SNOW** is gone, and then she pulls back the curtain. She peers deeply into the **MIRROR**, sees nothing, and then looks even closer. She rubs it a bit.)*

BELLE. Yoooo, hooo…anyone home in there?

> *(**SNOW** comes flying back in.)*

SNOW. Oh, she's gone out of control, who knows what she – Belle!

BELLE. What's the big deal?

SNOW. *(Stalks over to the **MAGIC MIRROR** and slams the curtains shut.)* I'm warning you, Belle, stay away from that mirror!

BELLE. Well how the hell am I supposed to powder my nose?

SNOW. If you're going to stay here, you'd better respect my rules.

BELLE. I don't know why you gotta be so selfish. Why can't I get a few wishes too?

SNOW. It doesn't grant wishes. It answers questions. Now I don't want to discuss this any further. My nerves are a frazzle.

BELLE. How bout a couple a shots of that royal mead?

SNOW. *(Pours two glasses of mead.)* Oh, Belle. What's happened to all of us?

BELLE. We got old, kid.

SNOW. We are not old, you have to stop saying that.

BELLE. It's true.

SNOW. I am twenty-nine, and you know it.

BELLE. For about the sixteenth time.

SNOW. Belle, how could you!

BELLE. But doll. Ya know what? You're still the fairest.

(She clinks her glass of mead to SNOW's.)

SNOW. R-really? Do you mean it?

BELLE. Sure do, baby. Now chin up. We've got us a party to throw.

(CINDY barrels back in holding a big sack of groceries. Her feet are bare and covered in blood-soaked bandages.)

CINDY. Ya want something done right, ya gotta do it yourself.

BELLE. Found your royal creamy poofs, did ya?

CINDY. And I told them to send you the bill.

BELLE. Pay your own bill, sister. I got a castle in foreclosure.

CINDY. *(Exiting into the kitchen.)* Snow, I'm just gonna drop this wild boar in your oven.

SNOW. Well, all right, I guess.

BELLE. Send me the bill. King Midas couldn't pay her dinner bill.

SNOW. She's smeared blood all over my royal tiles!

(She starts to clean it. The door bell rings.)

Ohhh, now what?! Belle, please!

BELLE. *(Goes to the door.)* All right, all right.

(She flings it open. There stands CHARMING. He is an absolute hunk. When he speaks, he will have the voice of a cool-as-a-cucumber mobster. BELLE doesn't recognize him and she immediately goes into flirt mode.)

Well! Hellllooo, sailor!

CHARMING. Hey, it's Belle! Howya doin' dollface?

SNOW. *(Picks herself up off the floor.)* Charming?

CHARMING. Snow! Bumpkin! Ya look like a million bucks!

BELLE. *(Confused.)* Charming?

CHARMING. Ya were expecting the Queen a Hearts?

BELLE. Oh my God, Snow, it *is* him!

SNOW. Charming you look so…so…

BELLE. – Absolutely gorgeous! Give a girl a hug, muffin.

> *(They hug. She's feeling all over his body.)*

CHARMING. Good to see you too, Belle.

BELLE. *(Feeling all over his arms.)* Ohh, Snow, call the cops. Two pythons escaped from the zoo.

SNOW. Belle, for goodness sake –

BELLE. What were they feeding you in that jail, honey? I barely even recognize you.

CHARMING. Ain't nothin' to do in the big house, baby. So me and Mustache Pete and Mickey the Mouse became workout partners.

BELLE. And boy, did it work out.

CHARMING. Hey, thanks for noticing. You ain't so bad yourself, toots.

BELLE. Ohhh, Charming.

CHARMING. And how you doin', Snow?

SNOW. Well…

CHARMING. Where's my old pal, Prince John?

SNOW. Ohhh. Well he, uhh… I mean… What I mean is… Perhaps I'd better go check the stove!

> *(She runs off in a tizzy.)*

CHARMING. Was it something I said?

BELLE. Well ya see…six years ago, ol' John went out for a bucket of milk…

CHARMING. Ahhh, the ol' bucket of milk routine.

BELLE. She's in complete denial, of course. Still thinks he's coming back. I heard a rumor that he's shacked up with the three pigs.

CHARMING. I always had a feeling he was a kinky bastard.

BELLE. *(She pours him some mead and refills her own glass.)* Snow's still skippin' all over the palace, singing to the birds and the mice. Between you and me, I think she's lost her marbles.

CHARMING. I don't know how many marbles were there to begin with.

BELLE. *(Clinks glasses with* **CHARMING**, *laughing.)* Oh, Charming, you always were a card. Speaking of which… did you really sell Alice to that deck?

CHARMING. Now let's not go dredgin' all that up again. I'm a changed man, Belle, or haven't you heard?

BELLE. Well, I think the old bag might be holding a grudge.

CHARMING. Ah, forget her. What about you, angel face?

BELLE. Me?

CHARMING. You still hooked up with that beast?

BELLE. As a matter of fact, I've left Bruce just today.

CHARMING. *(Puts his arms around her.)* Well, whadaya know? I always thought you deserved someone a little more… charming.

BELLE. Charming, you devil, you're a married man!

CHARMING. *(Releases her.)* Ah, you're right, Belle, I'm sorry. I just been in the clink ten long years, and I'm on fire.

BELLE. Are you ever.

CHARMING. So where is the little lady?

BELLE. Ahem. I believe the "little" lady is helping Snow in the kitchen.

CHARMING. *(Loudly.)* Aye! Cindy! What kind of welcome home is this? Where you at?!

            *(**SNOW** runs out.)*

SNOW. We're just putting the finishing touches on the feast.

CINDY. *(From the kitchen.)* Is that my deadbeat husband?!

SNOW. Oh dear…

> **(CINDY** *comes stomping out, a big goblet of mead in one hand and a creamy poof in the other, a big glob of cream on her chin… They stare at each other. Silence, then:)*

CHARMING. *(Utter horror.)* Cindy!

CINDY. *(Utter lust.)* Charming!

CHARMING. *(Utter horror.)* What happened to you?!

CINDY. *(Utter lust.)* What happened to you?

CHARMING. *(Utter horror.)* What's that in your hand?

CINDY. *(Utter lust.)* What's that in your pants?

SNOW. *(Taking the poof and the mead from* **CINDY***.)* Now Cindy why don't you put this down and go give your truly beloved a big welcome home hug.

CINDY. *(Stomping over.)* Don't mind if I do.

> *(To* **BELLE***, who is right next to him.)*

Beat it, bitch.

> **(CINDY** *goes to wrap her arms around him, and* **CHARMING** *recoils.)*

CHARMING. AHHHhhh, now, Cindy you know how I feel about public displays.

CINDY. *(Dangerous.)* Ya got some kinda problem?!

CHARMING. No, no. No problem. I just…wasn't expecting… so much of you.

CINDY. So! That's it, is it?

CHARMING. It's just that –

CINDY. Ladies, would you mind excusing us, I'd like a private word with my husband, as it were.

CHARMING. Uh, no need for that, we're all friends here.

CINDY. *(Roars at* **SNOW** *and* **BELLE***.)* I said SCRAM!

BELLE. *(Deadpan.)* You have creamy poof on your chin, dear. Third one from the bottom.

SNOW. Belle!

BELLE. Stop Belle-in' me, and come on. And grab that bottle of mead.

(They exit.)

CHARMING. Now listen, Cin –

CINDY. No, you listen, you sorry sack of shit and listen good! My life has been a complete and utter hell ever since you shoved that slipper on my foot!

CHARMING. What're you, nuts? You were nothing but a scullery maid before I saved you.

CINDY. Next time, don't bother. I'd rather suck corn from an elephant's ass!

CHARMING. Looks like you been doin' a lot of that already.

CINDY. Oh, that's right. I'm not ashamed. I've put on a pound or two

CHARMING. A pound or two? Can you get through the castle door without greasing it?

CINDY. *(Rages toward him.)* I oughta grease you, you son of a bitch!

CHARMING. Relax, doll. It's clear this little fairy tale of ours has come to an end. Why prolong the agony? We'll just ride the pumpkin on over to the kingdom clerk tomorrow and put in for the divorce. After all, we both got other options worth explorin'.

CINDY. I suppose you're referring to that red-headed halibut!

CHARMING. You leave Ariel out of this.

CINDY. Ohh, she's out of it, Charms, baby, don't you worry.

CHARMING. What's that supposed to mean?!

CINDY. Why nothing, my darling prince. Nothing at all. She's not been seen anywhere in the kingdom these ten long years, that's all.

CHARMING. What've you done with her?! I'm warnin' you –

CINDY. Whatever could I have done? I for one can't stand fish. Can't stand to be around it. It stinks! You're the one with a taste for the sea.

CHARMING. If you did somethin' –!

CINDY. *(Taunting him.)* Nevertheless, you'll recall I put my personal prejudice aside and for your last meal before they hauled you to the clink, I cooked you the most delightful seafood feast. Ohh, how I slaved in that kitchen for you. *Carving* and *chopping* that awful stinking *fish*. All. Day. Long. I felt just like I was back with Stepmother again. Covered in slime and scales. Just like the ones I found in our royal marital bed.

CHARMING. *(A slow realization.)* You couldn't have!

CINDY. But it was all for you, darling, and I liked it. I liked it. As did you, if memory serves. Ate every bite of your chopped chowder and your seared *red* snapper. Of course, your favorite part was the clam!

> *(**CHARMING** collapses in a chair, about to throw up.)*

Don't you worry! That was one fat fish. The royal freezer is filled with leftovers. You'll have many years to eat it up yum with a side of tartar!

> *(**BELLE** and **SNOW** run back in.)*

BELLE. Jesus Christ, what's all the racket?

CINDY. Divorce! Ha! I'll never grant you a divorce. All those years I put up with your philandering with everything on land and sea. Not that I wanted you touching me with those spindly little arms that I could floss my teeth with! But look at you now. You're a stud! And you're mine. All mine.

CHARMING. *(Runs for the door.)* Oh my God!!

> *(He opens the door and there stands **ALICE**, crazy eyes, and wild grin. They stare at each other a moment, and then **CHARMING** screams and runs out past her, exiting. There is a moment of stunned silence, and then:)*

ALICE. Did he have to leave so soon? I was just about to poison the tea.

(Blackout.)

Scene Three

(A clearing in the woods.)

(Bright music up, and remains up throughout the following.)

*(**SNOW** enters with a basket. She is picking berries in the forest, skipping along.)*

(She stops, takes a deep breath of forest air, strikes a pose, opens her mouth, and titters out a few musical notes as if calling to her forest friends. She holds out her finger. No bird lands on it. She looks around. No animals have joined her.)

(She takes another deep breath, trying to stay joyful, and starts to go into some more la-la-las but at the last minute, she lets her happy face drop into a mask of disgust, and just expels air in a huff.)

(She plops onto the forest floor, looks around to make sure the coast is clear, and then opens her basket and pulls out a joint. She looks around again, and then lights it and inhales deeply. She's in heaven.)

(She takes another drag, and then opens her basket again and pulls out a big bottle of booze. Pops the cap. Takes a giant slug. Takes another puff of the joint before snuffing it out.)

(She puts the remains back in the basket, pulls out a bottle of pills, and pours a bunch of them into her mouth. She washes them down with another slug of hooch.)

(She takes a spray bottle out – a spray to the face and then under the skirt.)

(And with that, her little picnic is over. The disgust is off her face. She's all happiness and rose petals again. She puts the bottle back in her basket, dances off the forest floor, and trills some

high-pitched musical notes, as she skips out of the forest. All is well in the world again.)

(Blackout.)

Scene Four

(The drawing room of Snow White's castle.)

(The place is a mess. Gowns and crowns and general clutter all over the place.)

(SNOW enters from her berry picking expedition. She is all sing-songy until she sees the mess, at which point she throws down the basket in exasperation.)

SNOW. Oh, for goodness sake. Belle, this is getting simply ridiculous!

(BELLE enters from the kitchen in her royal slip, holding a big chalice of mead. She's been hitting the sauce today, and it shows.)

BELLE. What are you squawkin' about this time?

SNOW. Look at this place! You can't keep throwing your gowns all over my royal floor.

(SNOW will clean the whole mess during the following.)

BELLE. Have the help pick it up.

SNOW. Belle, we've been through this. I've had to let the servants go.

BELLE. So *us* two old maids are the only ones left, huh?

SNOW. Stop calling me that! I am a happily married woman.

BELLE. Oh wake up and smell the break up, lady. It's all over town that he's rockin' it with those three pigs.

SNOW. You stop it this instant. Just because your marriage is –

BELLE. *(Laughing, pouring herself more mead.)* If he likes swine so much, maybe we should hook him up with Cindy. Does he want three little pigs, or the Queen Sow?

SNOW. I won't listen to another word of this, Belle.

BELLE. Fine by me if ya wanna live in denial. To get your mind off it, why don't you brew me up another batch of this here honey wine.

SNOW. How can I when you've drunk so much of it already that the royal honeybees have ceased production and fled the palace?! When did you become such an inebriate?

BELLE. I got problems.

SNOW. We all do, Belle, but pull yourself together or we're going to have to think about other arrangements.

(She exits with armfuls of **BELLE**'s *clutter.)*

BELLE. I got an arrangement for you, ya ol' bat.

(She staggers over to the curtained mirror and pulls back the drapes. She rubs it a little bit.)

Yooo-hooo…

(No response.)

I know you're in there, come out and play.

(She bangs on it hard. A puff of smoke and the mysterious face appears.)

MAGIC MIRROR. What the hell are you pounding this glass for?! How 'bout I come out there and pound on you?!

BELLE. *(Seductively.)* Ohhh, baby, I like it rough. Pound away.

MAGIC MIRROR. *(Confused.)* Wait – what? You're not Snow White.

BELLE. Not the last time I looked in a mirror.

MAGIC MIRROR. Listen, lady. You gotta get me outa here. She's crazy, I tell ya.

BELLE. Anyone ever tell you, you're kinda cute?

MAGIC MIRROR. Lady, listen. I can't take it anymore. She conjures me up with that sing-songy voice, day in, day out: "Who's the fairest?" "Am I the fairest?" "Why can't I be the fairest?" What am I, her beauty consultant?!

BELLE. What about me? Maybe I'm the fairest.

MAGIC MIRROR. Oh my God, you're all insane! Do me a favor and kill me now. Find a brick and shatter me into a million pieces!

BELLE. I wouldn't dream of it, dumplin'. Say, I never dated a head before. Wanna go steady?

> *(The* **MAGIC MIRROR** *screams and the face disappears in a puff of smoke.)*

Sheesh, I never knew mirrors were so sensitive.

> *(***SNOW*** flies back in, catching her red-handed.)*

SNOW. Belle!

BELLE. *(Innocently.)* What?

SNOW. That's it, Belle. I've warned you!

BELLE. Ya know, you've really turned into a shrew in your old age, and that mirror thinks you're bananas.

SNOW. This is the thanks I get for taking you in at your time of despair!

BELLE. Oh, yank the cork outa your ass!

SNOW. You've left me no choice. I want you to collect your things and leave my palace immediately.

BELLE. Now wait a second –!

SNOW. I'm sure Bruce will take you back.

BELLE. Take me back?! I ain't goin' back to that stinking musk ox and his pack of chinchillas.

> *(The doorbell rings.)*

That's probably him right now, desperate and drunk!

SNOW. *(Going to the door.)* Good, then you'll have something in common!

> *(She flings the door open, and there stands* **BRIAR ROSE***, a.k.a.* **SLEEPING BEAUTY***. She is dressed in pristine princess garb, and holds a small suitcase. She is absolutely gorgeous. She is the same age as the other princesses, but doesn't look a day over thirty. When she speaks, she will do so with an affected sophistication, sort of like Madonna, when she tries to be British.)*

ROSE. Snow. Darrrling.

SNOW. Oh my goodness! Belle, look!

ROSE. *(Kisses her on the cheek and waltzes into the room.)* It's been years, and dear, dear, dear Belle is here too? What an absolute gift.

BELLE. Well, well. If it ain't the sleeping beauty herself. Miss Briar Rose.

ROSE. Ah, that's Princess Rose, my dear, lest we forget.

BELLE. Yeah, well, I see they finally let you out of Celebrity *Princess* Rehab.

ROSE. Indeed they did, and Snow, dear, I'm afraid I need a place to stay –

SNOW. Oh, but I –

BELLE. What about Prince Philip?

ROSE. Don't be coy, Belle, it's never been your strong point.

BELLE. Yeah, that's right, everyone knows.

SNOW. Knows what?

ROSE. *(Teary.)* It's true. Philip didn't wait for me to finish my recovery. All these years, and now I'm off the booze and dope, only to find that he's taken up with that heathen temptress from the Middle East.

SNOW. Princess Jasmine?

BELLE. What are you, living in a hole? He's been ridin' Jazzy's magic carpet all over town.

ROSE. It's true. Oh, it's true. Leave it to me to pick the prince with a secret taste for baba ghanoush.

BELLE. We didn't pick much better, sister.

ROSE. Why, whatever do you mean?

BELLE. Bruce lost his job and became a no-good drunken layabout, and Snow hitched her wagon to a pig fucker.

SNOW. Belle!

BELLE. Snow's been dumped, I'm headed to divorce court, and Alice has lost her goddamned mind. I tell ya, those happy endings ain't what they used to be.

ROSE. Well. It seems I missed quite a bit whilst away. What about Cindy?

BELLE. That woolly mammoth is the only one still married...for now.

ROSE. Woolly mammoth?

SNOW. Um, what Belle is trying to say, Rose, is that Cindy has put on a few pounds.

BELLE. A few pounds? The bitch has more rolls than the royal bakery!

ROSE. Oh, dear.

BELLE. *(Heads to the kitchen.)* Back in a few. I'm gonna ransack that kitchen for another bottle of hooch.

(She exits.)

ROSE. Well. Quite a mouth that one's developed.

SNOW. Ohh, Rose. I simply don't know what to do with her anymore.

ROSE. Why must you do anything at all?

SNOW. Because she's left Bruce and moved herself in here. Three long weeks and all she does is drink and tell everyone to fuck off.

ROSE. Well, I myself shan't be any sort of trouble. I'll require an upper level suite overlooking the kingdom, of course, two hand maidens, and a chamber maid.

SNOW. But Rose...

ROSE. I'm used to breakfasts promptly at sunrise, and please inform the kitchen staff that I prefer fowl over fish for the evening banquets.

SNOW. Rose, you don't understand. There are no hand maidens. There is no staff.

ROSE. Of all the nonsense. Whatever do you mean?

SNOW. I've had to let everyone go, Rose. A dark recession has swept the land.

ROSE. Darling, we're royalty. None of that applies to us.

SNOW. I'm afraid it does. Prince John has been...lost, and it seems the royal bank account contains only cobwebs.

ROSE. *(Annoyed.)* No hand maidens?! Well who the hell's gonna rat my hair?

SNOW. But Rose, look at you. You're gorgeous. You don't need anyone to help with that.

> **(BELLE** *re-enters with more mead. This time she'll drink straight from the bottle.)*

ROSE. Really? Do you really think so?

SNOW. Of course I do. Honestly, it's as if you haven't aged a day. Your beauty is simply timeless.

BELLE. Yeah. It could stop a clock.

SNOW. Of course, lovely as you've remained, I'm still the fairest. It's a curse, really, to be so exquisite. The Queen nearly took my life for it. Now, I spend hours every day in front of the mirror admiring my allure. Oh, Rose. Do you think that's vanity?

BELLE. Naw. It's imagination.

ROSE. Belle, dear, what a tart little tongue you've developed. Perhaps that's why darling Bruce left you.

BELLE. I left him 'cause he's a no good drunk! *(She drinks.)*

ROSE. I can't imagine that to be the case. He was always such a good and kind man. And so very, very attractive. Rippling flank muscles and the most enchanting raven black hair all down his back.

BELLE. Too bad it ain't connected to his head.

ROSE. Nevertheless, if indeed he's single now, perhaps I'll call on him.

BELLE. *(Storms over to her.)* Now wait just a second you snooty old bat –

ROSE. Belle, dear, seeing you so close, I think you may have had some work done.

BELLE. So what if I have?

ROSE. Did you happen to keep the receipt?

SNOW. Now ladies, this is no way to behave on Rose's first day back from rehab. Let's all try to get along and act our age.

BELLE. If this one acts her age, she'll turn to dust and blow out the window.

SNOW. *(Tries to take the bottle from* **BELLE**.*)* Belle, I think you've had enough.

BELLE. Try grabbing that bottle again and you'll pull back a bloody stump.

ROSE. *(Exiting.)* In any event, I'll now retire to my chambers to get out of these travelling clothes and slip into something more comfortable.

BELLE. *(Yells after her.)* Why don't ya try slippin' into another coma?!

SNOW. Belle, what in the world is wrong with you?

BELLE. I should ask you the same thing. What're you, starting a boarding home for wayward princesses?

SNOW. Oh, Belle, I have a confession to make. I'm so terribly troubled.

BELLE. What's eatin' ya this time, pally?

SNOW. You see, I was chatting with the mirror, and he said… Oh it's so shameful. He said there's one fairer than I. Oh, Belle, do you think it's Briar Rose?

BELLE. That thing? Her face clearly went up in flames and someone tried to douse it with a pitchfork.

SNOW. Belle. You're just jealous is all. She's stunning.

BELLE. I'm stunned all right. I never could stand that dame. How dare she say she's gonna call on Bruce!

SNOW. But you're getting divorced.

BELLE. I'll lock him in a crate before I let Rose get her claws on him.

    (The doorbell rings.)

SNOW. Let me go check on her. Oh dear, Belle, will you get the door?

    *(***SNOW*** exits. ***BELLE*** staggers over to the door and flings it open. It is ***CHARMING***, totally frazzled. He has a broken chain on one hand.)*

CHARMING. *(Runs in, looking around madly.)* Is she here? Is she here?!

BELLE. Well hello to you too, big boy.

CHARMING. Cindy's gone nuts, I tell ya. She's had me chained to the bed for three days!

BELLE. I can understand the impulse.

CHARMING. My lawyer served her with divorce papers and she went batshit! She's wrecked the entire palace and she won't stop frying… *(His voice catches a little.)* …fish sticks.

BELLE. Fish sticks?!

CHARMING. Ohh, Belle, you don't know what she's capable of, and it's not just her! On my way over here, Alice tried to clock me with a pink flamingo!

BELLE. That hag needs electroshock.

CHARMING. You've gotta hide me! Jesus Christ, it was safer in jail.

BELLE. *(Nuzzling up to him.)* That's where you'll be if the coppers see you walkin' the streets with these two guns.

CHARMING. *(Getting turned on.)* Yeah, ya like that, do ya?

BELLE. Do I ever. Oh, honey, get outa that awful marriage and into my panties.

CHARMING. Be careful baby, I ain't been with a woman in ten years. I'd do horrible things to your vagina.

BELLE. Prove it.

CHARMING. Ohh, baby you're turning me on.

BELLE. Then come on up to my boudoir and you can ring my bell.

CHARMING. I'm ready to ring some bells, all right. Last night, I dreamt that I was with the most beautiful woman in the kingdom.

BELLE. Really? How did I look?

> *(**ROSE** enters, changed out of her former gown into a sexy and revealing nighty. **CHARMING** sees her and instantly tosses **BELLE** aside.)*

CHARMING. Just like that.

ROSE. Charming. Darling.

BELLE. I thought it was a dream, not a nightmare.

CHARMING. *(He's totally forgotten* **BELLE.***)* Briar Rose. The last time I saw you, you were amped out on angel dust with Flora, Fauna, and Merryweather.

ROSE. It's true. The three good fairies led me down a darkened path. Crack whores, every one.

BELLE. I hear they're lookin' for a roommate.

ROSE. *(Pushes past her.)* Of course now I'm clean and rested and ready to begin my life anew.

CHARMING. Ain't dat a coinkidink? I'm ready for some new beginnings myself.

ROSE. Tough times at the Cinderella castle?

CHARMING. Cindy and I are through. She just ain't quite accepted it yet.

ROSE. You don't say. What an unexpected development.

BELLE. Rose, dear, I realize that manners were never your strong point, but Charming and I were having a private conversation. After your long day of travel don't you need to get some *beauty* sleep?

ROSE. I've slept enough to last a lifetime, darling. I may never sleep again. You, on the other hand, might benefit from a nice hibernation.

*(*SNOW *runs on.)*

SNOW. Rose, I've cleared out the bedchamber you wanted –

ROSE. Got those rats out of there?!

SNOW. They aren't rats, they're squirrels, Rose, and all of my woodland friends are welcome here.

ROSE. If another one jumps through that skylight, I'll welcome it into a stewpot.

SNOW. Oh!

ROSE. Charming, don't you want to come take a tour of my chamber?

BELLE. As I said, we were having a –

CHARMING. I'd love to check out your chamber, baby.

ROSE. How wonderful. You'll find it's the moistest one in the castle.

> *(They exit.* **ROSE** *shoots* **BELLE** *a triumphant glance on her way out.)*

BELLE. *(Enraged.)* Who the hell does that tramp think she is?!

SNOW. Ohh, Belle, she made me move out of the master suite. She wanted it all to herself.

BELLE. You doormat! You gave it to her? I'd let her sleep in a horse stable!

SNOW. Oh dear. What if she hurts the squirrels?

BELLE. The only animal she's concerned with right now is *beaver*!

SNOW. Ohh, I don't think she should stay here.

BELLE. Yer damned tootin'!

SNOW. But how do we get her to leave? What do we do?

BELLE. You can do whatever the hell you want. I'm gonna go stand naked in her doorway holding a knife.

> *(She exits.)*

SNOW. Ohhh!

> *(She runs to the* **MAGIC MIRROR** *in distress.)*

Mirror, mirror that I stole from the –

> *(The mysterious face appears instantly.)*

MAGIC MIRROR. What? What? WHAT is it this time?!

SNOW. Mirror!

MAGIC MIRROR. Can't a disembodied head get some sleep around here?!

SNOW. But Mirror, you said another was the fairest. I must know. Is it Briar Rose?

MAGIC MIRROR. What the fuck is a Briar Rose?!

SNOW. So it isn't her?

MAGIC MIRROR. How the hell should I know?

SNOW. But you said –

MAGIC MIRROR. I said, I said. Lady, I'm a pathological liar!

SNOW. What?!

MAGIC MIRROR. I've never told the truth in my life!

SNOW. But of course you have. All those years when you said I was the fairest!

MAGIC MIRROR. The fairest? Ha! Is that your head or did your neck just vomit?

SNOW. Mirror!

MAGIC MIRROR. Don't worry toots! Looks ain't everything. In your case, they ain't anything!

SNOW. Oh my god!

MAGIC MIRROR. I'm kidding. I'm kidding. You've got a face like a flower.

SNOW. I do?

MAGIC MIRROR. A cauliflower!

> *(The **MAGIC MIRROR** cackles hysterically, and **SNOW** runs toward the front door in anguish.)*

Come back anytime! I got a million of 'em! I'm here all night!

> *(The **MAGIC MIRROR** cackles again and disappears. **SNOW** opens the door, about to run out, but before she can do so, **CINDY** barrels through, enraged.)*

CINDY. Where is he?!

SNOW. Cindy, this is not the time. My mirror has gone psychotic!

CINDY. I know he's in here! Alice saw him headin' this way!

SNOW. Do you know any doctors who can treat a looking glass?

CINDY. Listen you little simp. I wanna know where my bastard husband is and I wanna know now!

SNOW. It's not my job to keep track of your prince, now if you'll excuse me –

CINDY. And where's Belle?! I saw her givin' him the fish eye yesterday! If only she knew what happened to the last fish!

SNOW. Cindy, I'm asking you to leave. I'm very cross with you.

CINDY. Whadaya mean, you're cross?!

SNOW. I tried to throw you a perfectly lovely party and you ruined the whole thing!

CINDY. The next time I'm in the mood to have a party full of lettuce and fruit, I'll go have lunch with Bambi!

(There is a loud moan of ecstasy offstage.)

What was that?!

SNOW. What was what?

CINDY. That sound. I heard something. Who else is here?!

SNOW. Why, no one, I'm sure it's just my mirror about to go on another rampage, now if you'll –

ROSE. *(Voice, offstage.)* Not on my face! Not on my face!

(Pause.)

I SAID NOT ON MY FACE!!

CINDY. Who the hell is that?!

SNOW. Well I –

CINDY. *(Barreling off, toward the noise.)* If I find out you bitches are harboring a fugitive –!!

(She exits.)

SNOW. Cindy, wait!! Ohh, dear.

(There is a crash offstage, as if a door has been busted in, followed by some muffled commotion. Then:)

CINDY. *(Offstage.)* What is THIS?!

*(**SNOW** stands hysterically tearing at her hair as more clatter and commotion reign offstage. Then **CINDY** stomps back into the room. She stares at **SNOW** wildly.)*

Well, well.

SNOW. Cindy, I can explain.

CINDY. What kinda castle are you running, old woman?

SNOW. I will have you know I am twenty-nine!

> (**BELLE** *and* **ROSE** *slink on, wrapped in nothing but a sheet.*)

CINDY. Well, look what I found, Snow. Two princesses doin' the horizontal bop.

ROSE. *(With icy disgust.)* I assure you it's not what it seems.

CINDY. *(Acknowledging them.)* Hello Belle. And, my, my, my. If it isn't Briar Rose.

ROSE. Cynthia.

CINDY. It's been years and years. And don't you look just divine in Egyptian cotton.

ROSE. Why, Cynthia. How sweet. You're such a…well…a word hasn't been invented yet to describe what you are. But I assure you. You are one.

BELLE. And a big one at that.

CINDY. Now I don't suppose either of you has seen my beloved husband.

SNOW. I've already told you he's not here!

CINDY. Believe I was talking to the pussy bumpers.

BELLE. Now wait just a minute you rhinoceros!

CINDY. Oh, close your legs, Belle. I can smell your leftovers.

> (**CHARMING** *enters in nothing but his royal underwear. His hands are up. Behind him is* **ALICE**, *holding a pink flamingo before her like a loaded rifle.*)

ALICE. Look what I found hiding under the bed!

CINDY. Charming!

BELLE. How the hell did this batshit kook get in here?

ALICE. I turned myself small and floated in the window on a dandelion leaf. You'll never guess where I landed but it sure was big and it smelled like braggiole.

CINDY. I wanna know what's going on here, and I wanna know now!

CHARMING. Cindy, baby, relax –

CINDY. Don't you Cindy, baby me! Which one of you bitches is the goumada?!

ROSE. I beg your pardon!

SNOW. Really, Cindy –

CINDY. And as for you! Can the Little Miss Innocent act. You're clearly the ringleader of this entire charade!

CHARMING. All right, all right. Enough is enough already. Cindy. Baby. It's over.

CINDY. I warned you I'll never give you a divorce!

CHARMING. Oh, you'll give me a divorce, all right. Perhaps you forget that I'm connected.

CINDY. Don't you threaten me with your goon squad!

CHARMING. I'm just sayin'. I'd hate to have to ring up… Godmother.

CINDY. You leave Fairy Godmother out of this!

CHARMING. She's much more than fairy, baby. That broad is Capodecina. She's been runnin' the entire East Coast Syndicate for years.

CINDY. You're outa your mind.

CHARMING. Am I? Well she sure was fond of a certain mermaid I know of. If she knew what happened, she might have, shall we say, a little case of the vendettas, as it were.

BELLE. I don't know what either of you are talking about but this calls for popcorn and soda pop.

ROSE. *(Motions to* **CINDY**.*)* Don't give this one anything, dear. If she burps, she'll blow up the castle.

CINDY. How dare you! You're all in on it! You're all out to ruin me!

CHARMING. Relax, dollface. You can have the palace…and the horses…and the magic pumpkin.

CINDY. And where the hell are you gonna live?!

CHARMING. Well now. That depends.

> *(He pulls a ring out of his underwear and turns to* **ROSE**.*)*

Rose, baby. You're the one.

ROSE. Ohh, Charming.

CHARMING. Will you marry me?

BELLE. What?!

ROSE. Silly boy. You hardly know me.

CHARMING. Ask me anything.

> *(She covers his eyes.)*

ROSE. What color are my eyes?

CHARMING. Thirty-four D.

ROSE. I accept!

BELLE. Now wait just a goddamned minute here!

CINDY. You'll be sorry. You'll all be sorry for this!!

BELLE. I object to this turn of affairs! What about me?!

CHARMING. Don't worry, doll. I'll make you my goomah.

BELLE. I don't know what the hell that is, but I'll take it.

CHARMING. That's more like it. Now whadaya say we finish up our little party in the other room.

ALICE. Will there be tea?

BELLE. Beat it, bitch. This is a private affair.

CHARMING. Not so fast. That deck of cards tells me the dame's got skills.

> *(*BELLE *and* ROSE *exchange a look and shrug.)*

BELLE. Well, all right I guess.

ROSE. But only if she brings that flamingo.

CHARMING. Now you're talkin'. Hey there, Snow. Ya wanna join the festivities?

SNOW. *(Clueless.)* Ohh, I just adore festivities! Can I invite the squirrels?

CHARMING. What the hell. The more the merrier!

> *(They all start to head off together.)*

SNOW. What a delightful afternoon this has turned out to be.

CHARMING. Baby, if you three ain't walkin' with crutches by sunrise, I'll feel like I've failed ya.

(They exit. **CINDY** *stands alone.)*

CINDY. I'll kill 'em. I'll kill every last one of 'em!

(Smoke forms in the mirror.)

VOICE OF MIRROR. *(From behind the smoke.)* Why kill 'em… when you can curse 'em?

CINDY. What?! Who said that?

(The **MAGIC MIRROR***'s face appears.)*

MAGIC MIRROR. Over here, chickabiddy. On the wall.

CINDY. A magic mirror? Why, I've never seen a magic mirror before. Am I the fairest in the land?

MAGIC MIRROR. Jesus Christ!

CINDY. Well am I or what?!

MAGIC MIRROR. Yeah, yeah, you're all pretty. Now listen up. I gotta proposition for ya.

CINDY. I've never been propositioned by glass.

MAGIC MIRROR. Word on the street is you've been having a bit of, shall we say, marital discord.

CINDY. I think somebody's a fucking eavesdropper.

MAGIC MIRROR. Yeah, I heard the whole thing. Now listen. That bitch Snow White stole me from the Queen, and if I was a bettin' mirror, I'd bet ol' Queenie'd just love to dole out a little slice of revenge.

CINDY. You stupid head. The Queen's been dead for years.

MAGIC MIRROR. That's what they'd like you to believe. It sounds good in the fairy books. But I've got it on good information that the Queen is alive and well. In exile. On Evil Island.

CINDY. Evil Island?

MAGIC MIRROR. Along with every other villain who ever roamed the streets of the kingdom. You wanna get

back at Snow White and the rest of those floozies? Hop
the next barge to Evil Island and look for the Queen.

CINDY. What an absolutely delicious idea! You're a genius!

MAGIC MIRROR. She'll be glad to give you a nice curse, and
if not, one of those other broads is sure to have some
ideas. I'm sure they're all harboring grudges.

CINDY. Oh, thank you. Thank you! I'll leave at once. How
can I ever repay you?

MAGIC MIRROR. Just tell 'em…the mirror sent you.

(Poof! He disappears.)

CINDY. Evil Island! How wonderful. Those royal twats will
rue the day they ever fucked with Cinderella!

*(She cackles hysterically with an evil laugh, and
walks out the front door. As soon as she exists, there
is the sound of shattering glass. She has cracked
through another pair of slippers.)*

(Offstage.) Dammit!

(Blackout.)

End of Act One

ACT TWO

Scene One

(The shore of Evil Island; a dark night.)

(Foreboding music up.)

(Growls, grunts, caws, and other sounds of mysterious creatures fill the darkness.)

(An eerie fog [if possible] drapes the air.)

(The front of a rowboat pushes on stage. **CINDY** *splashes out of it, panting. Seaweed is around her neck. A lobster dangles from her gown, and a starfish is attached to her ass.)*

CINDY. Who the hell puts an island all the way in the middle of the ocean?!

(She rips the seaweed off her neck and hurls it off.)

What the –?!

(She sees the lobster clinging to her, screams, and yanks it off. Then she whirls around, sees the starfish, screams again, peels it off, and hurls it.)

(Center now, she hears growling sounds closing in around her.)

Who…who's there?! …Baba Yaga? …I come in peace… Is that you Big Bad Wolf? I… I always thought you got a bum rap.

(Suddenly, the sound of church bells replaces the growling and the sound of nuns chanting, such as the Chant from Avignon, *fills the air.)*

What's that? Sea Hag?? Maleficent??

(From the darkness, a **VOICE**.*)*

VOICE. What are these names you speak, my child?

CINDY. Who's there?! I don't want any trouble!

VOICE. There is no trouble here. Have you come to join the nunnery?

CINDY. Nunnery?!

(Lights rise slightly, revealing a **NUN** *sitting in front of a black cauldron, stirring slowly with a large wooden spoon.)*

NUN. The convent, my dear. I assume that's why you are here.

CINDY. Oh, uh, Sister, excuse me. I think I must've taken a wrong turn out by that lighthouse.

NUN. It's not an easy existence, to be sure, but I can see you're of fine stock and you've made up your mind.

CINDY. Now wait a second –

NUN. No need to wait. I'm Mother Superior, you see, and a flawless judge of character, if I do say so myself. You are clearly ready for a lifetime commitment to vows of poverty, chastity, and obedience.

CINDY. What are you, out of your fucking mind? I'm lookin' for Evil Island, not some house of prayin' penguins!

*(**CINDY** stomps back toward the boat.)*

NUN. What, may I ask, would bring, such a…petite flower… such as yourself to this so-called Evil Island?

CINDY. I gotta see the Queen!

NUN. The Queen of Hearts…?

CINDY. No, the one who tried to *eat* Snow White's heart. Now if you'll excuse me, I got some rowin' to do.

NUN. A moment, my child… What exactly do you want from this Queen?

CINDY. What's it to you, ya old bitch?

NUN. Just my holy curiosity, I suppose.

CINDY. Well as if it's any of your business, the mirror sent me.

(**CINDY** *is getting back in the boat.*)

NUN. *(Startled.)* Mirror?!

CINDY. You heard me, now go back to your poverty and chastity. I've gotta find Evil Island!

(**CINDY** *starts to row off.*)

NUN. *(Powerful.)* STOP!

(**CINDY** *stops.*)

You are already here. On Evil Island.

CINDY. You're off your rocker. I said evil. EVIL! Not a bunch of crones running around chanting at the moon!

NUN. *(Evil.)* I'll have you know that with one wave of my little finger I could draw every last breath from your bulbous body, crush your heart into blackened ash, and MAKE YOUR SKULL EXPLODE!!

(*There is a clap of thunder.* **CINDY** *stares at her.*)

That evil enough for ya?

CINDY. Hey, what's going on here?

NUN. If I thought you could pull all that blubber back up off the ground, I'd command you to kneel before the Queen!

(*She tosses back her wimple, revealing a crown.*)

CINDY. The Queen?

NUN/QUEEN. Did I stutter?

CINDY. Oh! Your, your Majesty! It is you! But what's with all this nun stuff?

QUEEN. It's all quite tiring, really, but this ridiculous exile on Evil Island has warped the brains of my former comrades. They've all grown to see the error of their former ways.

CINDY. So much that they formed a convent?

QUEEN. I'm afraid so. The Sisterhood of the Unhappy Ending.

CINDY. And they made *you* Mother Superior?

QUEEN. Why shouldn't they. I have the most crimes to atone for, after all. Attempted murder. Voyeurism. Harassment. Possession of a controlled substance. Produce poisoning. Who else should hold the position? Cinderella's stepmother? The only thing on that broad's rap sheet is unlawful imprisonment.

CINDY. My stepmother is here?!

QUEEN. *Your* stepmother?

CINDY. Don't you recognize me? I'm Cinderella.

QUEEN. You look like you ate Cinderella.

CINDY. Yeah well, looks like you left your fairest in the land days in the dust too sister.

QUEEN. Yes, yes, enough of this babble. Whatever are you doing here and what's this about my mirror??

CINDY. Your mirror? Ha! That thing's hangin' in Snow White's castle!

QUEEN. SNOW WHITE?!

(Another crack of thunder.)

What the hell is that sniveling bitch doing with my mirror?!

CINDY. Clearly she's nothing but a dirty crook.

QUEEN. I knew I should have slit her throat when I had the chance instead of fucking around with an apple!

CINDY. Any-hooo… The mirror says to tell you –

QUEEN. *(Suddenly tragic.)* The mirror… My mirror… Ohhhhhh…

(She collapses in a heap, sobbing.)

CINDY. Ahhmmmm, yes, well…forgive me for saying so but I don't know what the big deal is. It's just a bobbin' head inside a glass.

QUEEN. My dear. Clearly you have much to learn about the world. That "bobbing head," as you call it was a trusted friend…a compassionate confidante…and the most tender lover I have ever known.

CINDY. Ya don't say.

QUEEN. I'd give anything to see him again. To be held in the lustful gaze of my sweet, sweet speculum. To hear the soothing timber of his voice as he sings me songs of passion and amour. To feel his cold, ghostly tongue slither up the crack of my ass. Oh, can you help me?

CINDY. Help...you?

QUEEN. Oh, you simply must. Bring him to me.

CINDY. Lady, I ain't the Kingdom Courier! It's fifty miles to shore! You expect me to row another round trip just so some mirror can give a nun a rim job?!

QUEEN. You *will* bring him to me or I'll cast a spell that will make you rue the very day you were born!

CINDY. Wait a second, Nun. I thought you were out of the spell-casting business.

QUEEN. If you don't bring me that mirror, I promise I'll make an exception.

CINDY. How bout you make an exception, and I'll bring you the mirror.

QUEEN. Don't speak to me in riddles. What are you saying?

CINDY. Do you think I dropped over to this pile of rocks for cocktail hour? I'm lookin' for a curse!

QUEEN. A curse?

CINDY. That's right, and a good one too. I got four tramps who need to learn the meaning of the word *respect*!

QUEEN. I see. Revenge, is it?

CINDY. You better believe it, granny.

QUEEN. And who, pray tell, is the subject of your royal rage?

CINDY. Your little Miss Snow White, for starters. That slut's decided to throw herself a royal orgy, and my prince is the main course!

QUEEN. Oh dear. Infidelity is certainly worthy of a curse. I'm sure I could assemble something quite diabolical, especially for Ms. White.

(She goes back to the cauldron.)

CINDY. Now you're talkin'. And make sure you whip up a nice big batch. It ain't just Snow. I got all sorts of cursin' to do.

QUEEN. Silence! Now is the moment I shall summon all the powers of the underworld!

CINDY. Looks like someone's gonna be doin' a lotta Hail Marys tonight.

*(During the following, the **QUEEN** will hurl powders and potions from the pockets of her robe into the cauldron.)*

QUEEN. Graveyard ash, and coffin rust...

A heaping mound of mummy dust...

A witches bone, a scream of fright...

*(On "fright," the **QUEEN** grabs one of **CINDY**'s breasts and gives her a titty-twister. **CINDY** screams.)*

A blast of wind from darkest night...

A thunderbolt to mix it well...

Release the beasts from OUT OF HELL!!

(A gigantic clap of thunder is accompanied by a lightning bolt, and the growling sounds of furious creatures. More lightning. More thunder, and then silence. The lights return to normal as if nothing had ever happened.)

CINDY. Jesus Christ!

QUEEN. He had nothing to do with it, I assure you. And now, for your curse.

(She reaches into the cauldron, and pulls out a bright red apple.)

CINDY. What the hell is that?!

QUEEN. What the hell does it look like, you imbecile?

CINDY. You just got done telling me you were through with poison apples!

QUEEN. I should put your curse in a tenderloin steak?

CINDY. Works for me!

QUEEN. Clearly, in your sorry state of elephantine corpulence, you've forgotten the mindset of the simple princess.

CINDY. Corpu-what?!

QUEEN. This apple holds the symbol of greed, temptation, and sin. These are qualities no princess can resist. You simply tell your gaggle of harlots it's a magic wishing apple.

CINDY. Sounds too easy.

QUEEN. It works every time. They're all the same. One bite, and all their dreams will come true, blah, blah, blah.

CINDY. And then what? They all fall into the sleeping death? How'd that work out for ya last time?

QUEEN. Do you take me for a fool? This apple does not contain the curse of the sleeping death. This apple contains the curse of Aphrodite!

CINDY. The curse of Afro-what??

QUEEN. You fool. Aphrodite is the goddess of love, beauty, pleasure, and procreation. She was born when Cronus cut off Uranus's genitalia and threw them into the ocean, and she arose from the sea foam!

CINDY. Honey, something's starting to tell me you've been sittin' on those rosary beads too long.

QUEEN. Oh, but I assure you, it is a deliciously evil curse.

CINDY. Yeah, well all right, but I thought you'd zap me up something a little more snazzy than a piece of fruit.

(She grabs for it.)

QUEEN. Not so fast. A word about my payment.

CINDY. Payment?

QUEEN. My beloved mirror.

CINDY. Oh, that. Yeah, yeah, I'll bring you your Goddamned ass lickin' mirror.

(She yanks the apple out of her hand, stalks back to the boat, gets in, and starts to shove off.)

QUEEN. Be sure that you do. If it is not returned to me in two days' time, I'll send you a surprise that will make the sleeping death and the curse of Aphrodite look like a vacation in Bora Bora.

(She waves her hands in the air. Another huge thunderclap. Lightning.)

(Blackout.)

Scene Two

(The drawing room of Snow White's castle.)

(Late morning.)

(The doorbell is ringing, interspersed with some banging on the door.)

*(After a moment, **SNOW** runs in, looking frazzled.)*

(She wears a form-fitting bustier, and a pair of giant pumps that she can barely walk in. She runs to the door.)

SNOW. Oh dear… Coming…coming…

*(She flings the door open, and there stands **BEAST**, a.k.a. **BRUCE**. He is a bit more cleaned up than last time.)*

BRUCE. *(Startled by her outfit.)* Snow! Va-va-voom!

SNOW. Bruce! I wasn't expecting callers.

BRUCE. My God, what are you wearing?! I've never seen you like this!

SNOW. *(Realizes she is unclothed; runs and grabs a robe that hangs over a chair.)* Ohh dear… I'm sorry, I'm positively indecent.

BRUCE. *(Entering, shutting the door.)* Indecent? Those legs are the most decent thing I've seen all week!

SNOW. *(False modesty.)* Oh, come now.

BRUCE. I ain't kiddin', Snow. I never knew you were so… curvaceous.

SNOW. *(Lapping it up; letting a leg show flirtatiously through her robe.)* Really Bruce, you're embarrassing me. Now I suppose you're here to see Belle –

BRUCE. Well, uhh, yeah, but it seems you have a way of distractin' a person…

SNOW. Well, I just have no idea what you mean.

(She lets her robe "accidentally" fall off.)

Oh!

BRUCE. Ya know, somethin's different about you. If I didn't know any better, I'd say you were flirting with me.

SNOW. *(Putting the robe back on.)* Of all the nonsense. I don't flirt, Bruce, and I don't approve of people who do. Especially married men.

BRUCE. Married. Ha. I'm here to drop off the divorce papers Belle sent me.

SNOW. Ohh. You mean –

BRUCE. Yup. She really went through with it. After all I've done for her, she's left me high and dry and her kids to boot!

SNOW. Oh, Bruce, I'm so sorry. I've always adored your children. They have such lovely pelts.

BRUCE. Is Belle still stayin' here with you?

> *(Offstage,* **BELLE** *lets out a moan of passion.* **SNOW** *glances in that direction, concerned.)*

SNOW. Well, yes… Among others…

> *(Her mood suddenly changes. She bursts into tears.)*

BRUCE. Snow, dollface, what's with the waterworks?

SNOW. Oh, Bruce, you don't understand what it's been like over here. Ever since Belle moved in, my entire palace has been turned upside down.

BRUCE. She has a way of doin' that.

SNOW. It's not just her. Briar Rose is out of rehab and she's moved in too, but you see, it's not just that. Alice is always finding her way through a window or keyhole, and you might as well know it. Charming has left Cindy for good, and he's installed himself in the master suite, with Rose…and Belle…and Alice…and yes, I'll admit it, me as well! Oh, Bruce, we're practically his concubines!

BRUCE. To Charming? I always figured him a little light in the loafers.

SNOW. Ohh, he's not light in anything, Bruce, not light at all. It's heavy. Oh soo heavy.

BRUCE. Snow, it can't be.

SNOW. But it is. I'm a fallen woman, Bruce. Just your garden variety tart.

BRUCE. Not you. Never.

SNOW. We've done nothing but swing from the chandeliers morning to night, day after day, trying to sate an insatiable prince. Ohh Bruce. It feels like I have the weight of the world on my vagina.

BRUCE. I never knew what ten years in the clink would do to a guy.

SNOW. And on top of everything else, my magic mirror has popped a gasket and does nothing but hurl insults at me all day!

(The mysterious face appears in the mirror.)

MAGIC MIRROR. Hey Lady! Keep runnin' yer trap. Someday you'll say something intelligent!

SNOW. Oh! Go away! Go away!!

MAGIC MIRROR. But wait! I got an important message for ya!

SNOW. *(Concerned.)* A message? What kind of message?

MAGIC MIRROR. The zoo called! The baboon wants his ass back, so you'll have to find a new face!

(The **MAGIC MIRROR** *cackles hysterically.)*

SNOW. If you keep this up, I swear I'll shatter you to pieces!

BRUCE. Now listen here, Mirror! This is the royal princess Snow White, and you'll stop this abuse at once!

MAGIC MIRROR. Holy shit, what the hell are you?!

BRUCE. She is the mistress of this palace and you'll treat her with dignity and respect!

MAGIC MIRROR. Say, tell me something. Is that a beard, or are you chokin' on a muskrat?

BRUCE. Now wait just a minute here –

MAGIC MIRROR. The last time I saw somethin' that looked like you, I threw it a fish!

BRUCE. Why, I oughta –!

MAGIC MIRROR. That's all for now! Late show at ten! Two drink minimum!

> *(Poof! He is gone.)*
>
> **(SNOW** *burst into tears and collapses into* **BRUCE***'s arms.)*

SNOW. Oh, now do you see!? He's trying to drive me insane!

BRUCE. Snow baby, that piece of glass is clearly demented. Just look at you. You're a knockout!

SNOW. *(Swooning.)* Ohh, Bruce. Do you mean it?

BRUCE. Prince John must've been off his rocker to leave a dame like you.

SNOW. He's just out for a bucket of –

BRUCE. Enough small talk. Pucker up.

> **(BRUCE** *dips her grandly and kisses her with passion.)*
>
> **(ALICE** *slinks on in lingerie and pumps, her hair in pigtails like the girl from* The Bad Seed. *She also has three tits, having clearly drank the three titty tea. She lingers in the corner.)*

SNOW. But I – but you – but we –!!

BRUCE. Va-voom, that mirror is crazy. You're clearly the fairest of them all.

> *(And with that, she's his.* **SNOW** *is all over him. Kissing him wildly. Feeling him all over. They fall to the floor in passionate embrace.* **ALICE** *stalks over.)*

ALICE. Well, well, well.

> **(SNOW** *and* **BRUCE** *freeze and look up.* **SNOW** *screams.)*

What do we have here?

BRUCE. Uhh, hey there, Alice. How goes it, down in the rabbit hole?

ALICE. My hole's quite delicious. Thank you kindly for asking.

SNOW. Now Alice, this isn't what it looks like.

ALICE. How curious and curiouser. Things that don't look like what they are can be curious things indeed.

SNOW. Ahh, Bruce, maybe you should go.

(She shuffles him toward the front door.)

BRUCE. But I –!

SNOW. Yes, I think that's best, I'll…\I'll give Belle the papers.

BRUCE. But –!

SNOW. Thanks for stopping by, Bruce. Perhaps I'll call on you later.

(Slam. He is gone. She turns to face **ALICE** *who stares at her with an insane googly smile.)*

Now, Alice –

ALICE. I'm telling.

SNOW. Alice, really, let me brew a pot of tea.

ALICE. I already drank my tea! My three titty tea! Do you like my third titty? Isn't she pretty?

SNOW. Ahh, yes dear, she's, uh, adorable, now about what you saw –

ALICE. Ahhhhh. Yessssss. What I saw. I am going to tell!

SNOW. Alice, please, we really must talk this over –

*(***BELLE*** *stumbles in, also in sexy lingerie and pumps. She walks bow-legged and looks absolutely wrecked.)*

BELLE. Jesus Christ, what's all the racket in here?

SNOW. Oh, Belle, good you're up. Perhaps I'll get breakfast started.

BELLE. Screw breakfast. I need coffee. And where the hell have you been all night? Makin' me and Rose do all the work again?!

(There's coffee on the table and SNOW *serves it during the following.)*

SNOW. I was having a restful slumber like any normal person.

BELLE. Rest! I haven't had any rest in days. That Goddamned Charming is ravenous, and this goumada shit is gettin' old real quick. I can barely walk.

SNOW. Belle!

BELLE. I can barely stand up! It feels like my pussy's trying to claw its way out of my asshole wearing stilettos!

SNOW. Well, clearly this is too much for you. You simply must tell him.

BELLE. You think that egotistical son of a bitch is gonna listen to anything I have to say? Mr. God's Gift to Women don't know the first thing about the female anatomy! All he does is pound away like he's trying to knock down the palace door!

ALICE. I concur. And he doesn't even properly utilize my pigtails.

> (ALICE *opens her mouth wide and pulls her head forward several times with the pigtails.* BELLE *notices* ALICE *for the first time and recoils in disgust.)*

BELLE. Ain't you got a rabbit to chase?!

SNOW. This has all gone far enough. I'll talk to him with you, Belle, come on. Where is he?

BELLE. Last I checked he was flat on his back in the master suite with Briar Rose shovin' a bluebird up his ass.

SNOW. Bluebird what?!

ALICE. But of course. We ran out of chipmunks.

BELLE. You just keep them udders away from me, you freak! Those slimy nipples grazed my back last night, I thought it was a jellyfish attack!

ALICE. Charming seemed quite taken with my new breasticle.

BELLE. Yeah well clearly he'll bang anything with half a pulse if you're still floppin' around that bed!

SNOW. Just listen to yourselves! We've got to put a stop to this debauchery once and for all!

BELLE. Sing it, sister.

SNOW. We are all royalty here, or don't you remember, and this is no way for royalty to behave.

> (**BRIAR ROSE** *enters, decked out in dominatrix garb.*)

ROSE. Ahh, what a glorious morning.

BELLE. It was until now.

ROSE. Snow, darling, I'm simply famished. I'll have two farm fresh eggs, a slab of hickory smoked bacon, and a chocolate scone.

SNOW. Rose, I have told you time and again that the cupboards are bare. I'll be happy to pour you a cup of gruel.

ROSE. Honestly, Snow, the accommodations here are positively lacking. You can't possibly expect a woman of my stature to ingest something so commonplace.

BELLE. Then yank the bluebird outa Charming's ass and munch on that instead.

ROSE. Ahh, dear, dear Belle. Always a retort. Why don't we go back to bed and find a better use for that acid tongue.

ALICE. I have a secret.

ROSE. Kindly keep it that way, dear. No one wants to hear any more ravings from a demented psychopath.

ALICE. It's a very good secret, and I am going to tell.

SNOW. *(Shuffles her toward the door.)* Now, Alice, now is not the time, why don't you go visit the Caterpillar.

BELLE. Why don't you go play in the street!

SNOW. Alice run along, your Wonderland friends will be so pleased with your new appendage.

ALICE. I caught Snow White red-handed, I did! Right in this very room, I did!

SNOW. *(Pushes her out the door.)* Goodbye, Alice!

ALICE. Stroking and squeezing and fondling and –

> *(Slam. She is gone.* **SNOW** *turns to face the others.)*

SNOW. *(Flustered.)* Poor dear. I don't think she got enough oxygen at birth.

> **(CHARMING** *saunters on in an open robe and royal boxers looking quite pleased with himself.)*

CHARMING. Hey, hey, hey. Here they are. All my favorite girls!

BELLE. Oh, Christ.

CHARMING. Rose. *(He kisses her.)* Belle. *(He slaps her on the ass.)* Snow, baby we missed ya last night.

SNOW. I, I had a horrible headache.

CHARMING. Sorry to hear that, doll, ya missed a new position I like to refer to as the Twisted Sister Backdoor Bang.

SNOW. Yes well, this is just what I need to talk to you about.

CHARMING. Mind pouring me a cup a that joe?

SNOW. Yes, yes of course. Now the thing is… Well, I just feel… Well Belle and I feel… Well it just seems as though…

BELLE. Oh just spit it out! She wants to know if you're trying to fuck us all to death!!

CHARMING. Hey, now what are you talkin' about? I thought we was having ourselves a fine old time.

ROSE. Old is the key word when Belle is involved.

BELLE. Clearly you confused my yawning for an orgasm!

CHARMING. Yawning? You three have been screaming so loud I don't know if my name is Charming or God!

SNOW. All right, enough of this! Now we've all had our fun, but this entire palace has descended into a den of moral turpitude and I simply will not stand another minute of it.

ROSE. I concur, Snow dear. As fascinating as its been getting to know the freak show that is Belle's labia minora, my royal wedding is in three short moonfalls, and you two don't have time to be lazing about the castle like a pair of ancient cows.

BELLE. Oh, is that so?

ROSE. It certainly is so. You should both be hard at work on my imperial gown.

BELLE. I ain't makin' you no gown, bitch.

ROSE. Ohh, Snow, do you hear the way she talks to me? After all I've been through? Surely your little woodland friends could help a poor penniless princess have the wedding of her dreams?

SNOW. Well, Rose, to be honest, my woodland friends are all a bit…traumatized by the recent goings on.

ROSE. Traumatized? Why, whatever do you mean?

> *(A bluebird falls out of her ass and hits the floor with a thud. They all stare at her. She bends down and picks it up by its tail feathers, hands it to* **SNOW**.*)*

Ahh, yes, well… A little dip in the birdbath and he'll be good as new, you'll see.

SNOW. Ohh, dear…

ROSE. *(Takes* **CHARMING***'s hand and they head off.)* Come, Charming, darling. Let's dress and head to town to size our royal rings. Snow, I've taken some of your palace jewels for barter. I'm sure you don't mind.

SNOW. What –?!

ROSE. Toodles, girls. Now get to work on that dress. *(She snaps her riding crop.)* Use nothing but the finest silk and gossamer, as is fitting for one so fair!

> *(She exists with* **CHARMING**.*)*

SNOW. Ohh, dear… Belle, where are we going to find gossamer?

BELLE. We're not makin' her any dress, you simp! She can get married wearing a barrel for all I care!

SNOW. Ohhh, we'll have to go to the dungeon and visit the spider queen. Perhaps we'll convince her to loan us some silk. Come on!

BELLE. Are you off your rocker? I don't talk to no bugs!

SNOW. If we're hosting a grand wedding, we're going to do it right. And just think…it will finally get Briar Rose out of the palace!

BELLE. Which way to the dungeon?

SNOW. This way, but Belle, help me with something first.

*(She runs to the **MAGIC MIRROR**.)*

BELLE. What?

SNOW. Hurry, before it wakes up and starts taunting me again. I'll put it someplace no one will ever find it.

*(The two of them pull the **MAGIC MIRROR** off the wall.)*

BELLE. But Snow, honey, who's gonna tell you you're the fairest in the land?

SNOW. Perhaps I never was fairest in the land. Perhaps… and of course this is the more likely scenario… I always was and always will be…but either way…I've learned something important these past weeks. Beauty is only skin deep and all that really matters is…inner beauty.

BELLE. That's great, Snow, now come on let's get this over with before the wrinkle fairy pops by to do another tap dance on your face!

*(**SNOW** looks like she's been slapped, but before she can say anything, **BELLE** pulls her offstage, mirror in tow. A moment passes. Then, the front door slowly opens, and **CINDY** peeks in.)*

CINDY. Hello there…?

(She pushes the door open a bit more.)

Anybody home…?

(She creeps in, stealthily, and tiptoes across the room over to where the mirror once hung.)

CINDY. *(Cont.)* All right Queenie, I got your Goddamned ass-lickin' mirror.

(She reaches out for it, and sees that it is gone.)

What the –?! Where is it?

(She spins around wildly, looking in all directions.)

What have they done with it?

QUEEN'S VOICE. *(An echoey memory in* CINDY*'s mind.)* If the mirror is not returned to me in two days' time, I'll send you a surprise that will make the sleeping death and the curse of Aphrodite look like a vacation in Bora Bora.

CINDY. I'll get it! I'll get it! I've got it! I'll simply crash the wedding of Charming and his sleeping cootie, find out where they're hiding that mirror, and then serve up a few doses of Aphrodite's curse! Easy as pie. If all goes according to plan, four tramps will end their evening floating face down in the moat!

(She cackles hysterically.)

(Blackout.)

Scene Three

(The drawing room of Snow White's castle.)

(The evening of Briar Rose's wedding and royal ball.)

(Several trays of food and drink clutter the table. In the distance, the sound of waltz music can be heard, as well as the din of a large and boisterous crowd.)

(The front door opens and **BELLE** *barrels in, dressed in her finest gown. She is followed quickly by* **SNOW***, who holds the bridal bouquet.* **BELLE** *heads straight for the tray of drinks and snatches a cocktail. She'll knock them back throughout the scene.)*

SNOW. *(As they enter.)* Ohh, what a lovely wedding ceremony, don't you think, Belle?

BELLE. What the hell is the matter with you? You weren't supposed to boil the rice before you threw it!

SNOW. Well how was I to know? I've never arranged a royal wedding before.

BELLE. I'll be pickin' this outa my wiglet all night!

SNOW. *(Runs to look down the hallway.)* Ohh dear! The guests are already arriving in the ballroom! Where is Alice? She promised to help us out!

BELLE. Don't count on it. Bitch is high as a kite.

SNOW. Belle, please take it easy on the mead. It's going to be a long evening and I don't want any incidents.

(The front door opens and in strolls **ALICE***, in her usual dress.)*

BELLE. And where the hell have you been? Out trying to grow yourself a fourth tit?

ALICE. There's a line of horse-drawn carriages as far as the eye can see.

SNOW. Yes, yes, who knew Briar Rose was so popular… Ohhh, Alice, I asked you to wear your nice gown. This is a formal affair!

BELLE. And ya smell like the bottom of a bong!

ALICE. I want to thank you both most kindly for hiring me to host your little fête.

BELLE. Hire you?! I wouldn't hire you to haunt a house!

ALICE. Now about my payment –

SNOW. Oh, Alice, don't be silly, you know we have no money left, especially after this ball.

ALICE. But I simply must be compensated or I am going to tell.

SNOW. Please, Alice, not this again, the guests are all arriving at the ballroom entrance! Just go to the front and announce them as they enter!

ALICE. Payment in gold bullion coins should suffice –

SNOW. Yes, yes, whatever you say, just go!

(**SNOW** *pushes her off.*)

BELLE. You're really gonna let that pinhead near your guests?

SNOW. Well I can't do everything, can I, and don't get too comfortable, I need you to go out there and pass this tray of drinks!

BELLE. Do I look like a barmaid to you?

SNOW. I don't have time to argue, now just –

BELLE. Say, that was real impressive back there. You caught that bridal bouquet like a linebacker goin' for a touchdown.

SNOW. What?

BELLE. You broke Rapunzel's nose the way ya dove at that thing, and I'm pretty sure if you check the bottom of your shoe, you'll find Thumbelina.

SNOW. I can't help it if they got in my way!

BELLE. Just sayin' someone really wants to be next in line for a little holy matrimony.

SNOW. Belle, how many times do I have to tell you I am a happily married –

> (**ALICE** *enters with a horn, which she blows loudly.* **BELLE** *and* **SNOW** *both jump.*)

ALICE. Announcing the arrival of the royal incestuous siblings, Hansel and Gretel!

> (*She blows the horn again.*)

SNOW. Alice, for goodness sakes, I want you to announce the guests to the ballroom, not to us, now go, go, go!!

> (**SNOW** *shoves* **ALICE** *out of the room as the doorbell rings.*)

BELLE. Where the hell'd she get that tooter?

SNOW. (*Hands her a tray of drinks.*) You take this, now go serve!

BELLE. I need a nap.

SNOW. (*Pushing her out.*) And remember, they are for the guests, not you!

BELLE. But I –

SNOW. Go!

> (**BELLE** *exits. The doorbell rings again.*)

Ohh, dear…

> (**SNOW** *runs to the door.*)

What now??

> (*She flings the door open. There stands* **BRUCE**/ **BEAST**, *cleaned up, and holding a bouquet of flowers.*)

BRUCE. Va-voomsers! Snow, you're gorgeous!

SNOW. Oh! Ohh, Bruce, what are you doing here?

BRUCE. Here for the ball, of course… But I'm really here for you.

> (*He hands her the flowers.*)

SNOW. Oh, Bruce. You shouldn't have… And the ballroom entrance is on the other side of the –

(He kisses her deeply, dipping her back. She drops the flowers, giving in to his passion. She breaks away.)

SNOW. *(Cont.)* Oh, Bruce. We shouldn't. We oughtn't. We mustn't. We...

(She dives back in, kissing him madly. ALICE *enters with a gong. She is about to hit it, but when she sees what is happening, she freezes, and lingers silently in the corner, watching everything.)*

BRUCE. Snow. It's you. It's always been you.

SNOW. But what about Belle?

BRUCE. Belle? Ha! I never loved her! She's been a blithering shrew since the day I first locked her in my dungeon!

SNOW. Well, not all girls are into that kind of thing.

BRUCE. But you. Ohh, Snow. I knew our time would come.

SNOW. Well... I did catch the bridal bouquet today.

BRUCE. So I heard. And it's why I'm here. It's a sign, don't you see? Snow White, would you make me the happiest beast alive and be my bride?

SNOW. But... Prince John...

BRUCE. Baby, that good for nothing ain't been around for six years. In the eyes of the law, you're abandoned goods.

SNOW. Oh, I suppose it's true, isn't it?

BRUCE. It sure is. I know a lout like me don't deserve a hot dame like you, but do you think you could find it in your heart to ever love a beast?

SNOW. Ohhh, Bruce, I think I could!

(They start to kiss again, and ALICE *bangs the gong loudly.* BRUCE *and* SNOW *break apart instantly and turn to her.)*

ALICE. *(With a sly grin.)* Announcing the arrival of Princess Rapunzel!

SNOW. Oh!

ALICE. Her dress is by Chanel. Her tiara by Tiffany. And her bloodied bandaged nose courtesy of the House of Snow White.

SNOW. Alice, please, I asked you to –

ALICE. I hear she's planning on doing a little ass kicking.

SNOW. Bruce, um, why don't you be on your way. We can continue this later.

BRUCE. Why don't you pack up your things, and I'll pick you up after the ball for a little happily ever after.

SNOW. Oh Bruce, do you mean it?

BRUCE. Do I ever.

> *(He kisses her again, and exits.* SNOW *slams the door and turns on* ALICE.*)*

SNOW. Now listen here you little snoop –!

ALICE. Ah, yes. Now about my payment –

SNOW. Alice, there is nothing whatsoever to pay you with and you know it.

ALICE. Well ya better cough somethin' up, sister, or I'm gonna start singin' to the coppers.

SNOW. If you think anyone's going to believe one word that comes out of your mouth, you're the Queen of Crazytown!

ALICE. Maybe Belle will believe me.

SNOW. Now, Alice, please, let's be reasonable –

> *(BELLE comes flying back in. The tray is empty. She has one drink in the other hand, and it's not her first.)*

BELLE. That ballroom is teaming with hunks! Hey, Snow, your dwarves are here, and they've been takin' steroids!

ALICE. Oh, Belle, I have a most important piece of information just for you.

BELLE. Whadaya want, ya goon?!

SNOW. Alice, I told you we will work this out, now get back out to that ballroom and announce the guests!

ALICE. Gold bullion coins!

(**ALICE** *exits.*)

SNOW. Ohh dear, Belle, will you go see if Captain Hook is here and ask him if he can spare a few doubloons?

BELLE. I'm goin' on break!

SNOW. Fine, fine, well how does everything look out there? Do people seem to like Rose's gown?

BELLE. Define "like."

SNOW. You know, under the circumstances, I think we did a marvelous job on that dress.

BELLE. Rose may have had a difference of opinion when she was trying to set it on fire.

SNOW. Well, I don't know what she expected. We got her silk, just like she asked for, and that spider queen is a wonderful seamstress.

BELLE. Let's just say we don't have to worry about her giving us any more sewing assignments.

SNOW. Ohh, I suppose you're right.

BELLE. *(Sniffing, suspiciously.)* Say, what's that smell?

SNOW. What smell?

BELLE. That smell, that smell, like the inside of a dead polar bear's crotch! Bruce was here, wasn't he??

SNOW. No, no, I'm just baking some gruel into passed hors d'oeuvres is all.

BELLE. *(Grabs **SNOW**, sniffs her.)* It's you! Bruce's scent is all over you!

SNOW. Now Belle, you're mistaken, I must simply have forgotten to douche.

BELLE. What are you trying to pull, old woman? Are you fooling around with my husband behind my back?

SNOW. Your husband? But the two of you are through!

BELLE. I'll decide who's through, now what's going on here?

SNOW. Oh. Well, of course. How could I have forgotten? Bruce did stop by. To drop off your divorce papers. You're officially single now.

BELLE. *(A bit crestfallen.)* Oh.

SNOW. Well, what's the matter? I thought that's what you wanted.

BELLE. Ya know, Snow, honey. The truth of the matter is... I kind of miss the bastard.

SNOW. Miss him? But you hate him!

BELLE. Yeah, I know, but maybe I'll give him another chance anyway.

SNOW. Belle, I think that would be a terrible mistake.

BELLE. Or do what? Live out my days here with you as a coupla spinsters, singin' songs to the rats and the frogs?

SNOW. You're not thinking rationally, now just –

> *(**ALICE** enters with the gong, which she bangs loudly. **BELLE** and **SNOW** jump.)*

BELLE. Bang that one more time and you'll be wearin' it as a diaphragm!

ALICE. Announcing the royal princess Briar Rose!

SNOW. Alice, I've asked you to announce in the ballroom!

> *(**ALICE** exits with a huff.)*

ROSE. *(Offstage.)* But that announcement's for you, dear.

> *(**ROSE** stomps on. She is wearing her "wedding gown," which is a slinky and bizarre getup that appears to have been made entirely from spider webs. In fact, a few spiders adorn the gown. Everyone stares at her, and she is not happy.)*

SNOW. Oh, Rose, don't you look beautiful... Belle, doesn't Rose look pretty?

BELLE. Pretty as a picture, and I'd sure like to hang her.

ROSE. How delightful, I'm sure. Well, I just came to thank the two of you for making me the laughing stock of the entire kingdom!

SNOW. Now Rose, I know it's not a traditional look, but it's very fashion forward.

ROSE. Fashion forward?! I must be the first broad in history to get married wearing a spider web!

SNOW. You'll just have to trust me on this, Rose. It's very, very elegant.

ROSE. Yes, that's exactly what Tinker Bell was saying before she smashed into my ass.

> *(She turns around, revealing Tinker Bell, tangled in the webs around her butt.)*

BELLE. I'm sure it was impossible to avoid.

ROSE. In any case, better that my gown was sewn by an arachnid than by two sniveling cockroaches.

BELLE. Now wait just a Goddamned minute –!

> *(**CHARMING** enters.)*

CHARMING. Hey! Doll! What gives? We were right in the middle of the cha-cha-cha!

ROSE. If I cha-cha one more step, this disgusting rag is going to fly apart at the seams and then that party will get an eyeful of cha-cha that they weren't expecting!

BELLE. That oughta clear the dance floor.

> *(**ALICE** enters, bangs the gong.)*

ALICE. Announcing the royal princess, Cinderella!

BELLE. She's not on the guest list, you fool!

> *(**ALICE** exits as **CINDY** barrels on.)*

CINDY. Well, well, well. Isn't this a pretty sight.

> *(She walks slowly by the women, curtsying to each of them.)*

Belle… Snow…

> *(She gets to **ROSE** and stops in her tracks with a shudder.)*

Yeeeesh…!

SNOW. Cindy, what are you doing here?

CINDY. What am I doing here? Why, I'm here for the royal ball, of course. I for one love a ball, and what a brilliant assemblage you've gathered. All the royalty and nobility in the land... *(She sniffs at* **BELLE**.*)* ...and even the riff raff.

SNOW. Cindy, I'm sorry but I really need to ask you to –

CINDY. Naturally, I was ever so distraught not having received an invitation, but I'm sure it was simply lost in the mail.

SNOW. I'm afraid not, Cindy.

ROSE. That's right, dear. You weren't wanted.

CINDY. *(Mock surprise:)* Weren't wanted?! Oh my. What an awkward situation. I had hoped that it was due to some oversight. Oh well... I'd best be on my way.

SNOW. Thank you for being so mature about this.

CINDY. Oh. But before I go, how about one final parting kiss for my dear, darling beloved ex-husband?

ROSE. Beat it, bitch. He's mine, now.

CINDY. Well, of course he is, Rose dear, and you certainly deserve each other, but I still think one final kiss is in order don't you, Charming?

CHARMING. I'd rather get a blow job from a fire breathing dragon.

CINDY. I see. There's one in the Misty Mountains and I'd be happy to hook you up.

CHARMING. *(To* **ROSE**.*)* I'll see ya back on the dance floor, doll. It's a little too crowded in here for my taste.

(He kisses her, shoots **CINDY** *a glare, and exits.)*

CINDY. How lovely. Charming to the bitter end.

ROSE. Oh he's full of charm, I assure you, and by the end of the night, I plan to be full of him.

SNOW. Cindy, let me escort you back to your pumpkin.

CINDY. That's right, I'm leavin', I'm leavin', but to show you all I bear no hard feelings, I should like to bestow a gift.

BELLE. What kinda gift?

CINDY. This kinda gift!

(She whips out the apple and holds it high in the air.)

ROSE. *(With total disdain:)* Oh. Really. You shouldn't have.

CINDY. Yes, yes, I know what you're thinking. But this is no ordinary apple. It's a magic wishing apple. One bite and all your dreams will come true!

SNOW. This all sounds very familiar.

CINDY. *(Shoves it right in SNOW's face.)* Go on now, don't be shy. Have a bite!!

SNOW. *(Pushes her away.)* Now, Cindy, this is all very kind of you but I don't fool around with magic apples any more. The last one gave me a terrible stomach ache.

CINDY. Don't you have any dreams? What about your long lost husband all shacked up with those three swines down the hill? One bite could bring him back, and the two of you could have yourself a nice pig roast.

SNOW. No, no, the pigs can have him. I no longer want him back.

CINDY. Well there must be something! I'll have you know this apple was very expensive!

BELLE. *(Yanks the apple from her.)* I'll take a bite of that thing! I got a few wishes to make.

CINDY. Now you're talkin'!

ROSE. A few?! How much are you planning on eating?

BELLE. Just as much as I damn well please!

ROSE. *(Grabs it.)* I don't think so, darling, I need some new patio furniture for my castle in the clouds.

BELLE. *(Grabs it back.)* Well I ain't even got a castle or a prince to live in it!

ROSE. *(Grabs it back.)* Look in the nearest mirror and you'll see why!

CINDY. Ahhh, speaking of mirrors, Snow, honey, where's that delightful talking mirror that used to hang over on that there wall? He was so very sweet, and I'd love to say hello before I leave.

SNOW. Why, I, I don't know what you mean.

ROSE. *(Still fighting* BELLE *for the apple.)* Mirrors don't talk, you idiot!

BELLE. Lucky for you, they don't laugh either!

ROSE. You just give me that apple!

> *(*BELLE *takes a defiant bite.* ROSE *gasps, yanks it out of her hand and takes a big bite.)*

BELLE. *(Yanks it back.)* Why I oughta –!

> *(They struggle for it and it flies out of their hands and rolls offstage.)*

ROSE. You fool! Now look what you've done! The entire ballroom will think they're entitled to wishes!

> *(*ROSE *runs off after the apple.)*

BELLE. Get back here, you bitch! That apple is mine!

> *(*BELLE *runs off after* ROSE.*)*

SNOW. Ohhh dear!

> *(There is a loud cacophony off stage. Banging, clattering, etc.)*

ROSE. Get off of me, you're gonna tear my webbing!

BELLE. I'll rip it off your sagging bones if you don't give me that apple!

> *(More clattering, more banging.)*

SNOW. My, that must be a very fresh apple.

CINDY. Ahem. Yes, well… Now about that mirror…

> *(Suddenly, there is the sound of a small explosion offstage, like someone set off a firework. The lights flicker, and there is a poof of smoke where* BELLE *and* ROSE *exited that spills onto the stage.)*

SNOW. Oh no!

ROSE. *(Offstage, coughing.)* What, what's happening to me??

BELLE. I feel dizzy!

ROSE. I feel sick! I think I'm going to pass out!

CINDY. Yes! Yes! My diabolical plot has worked perfectly!

SNOW. Plot? Girls, are you okay??

> (BELLE *and* ROSE, *both looking totally dazed,*
> *stumble back on through the fading smoke. Instead*
> *of their normal hair, they now sport gigantic and*
> *ridiculous afros.* CINDY *and* SNOW *stare at them*
> *for a moment, and then* CINDY *starts laughing*
> *hysterically.*)

CINDY. Blaaa-hahahahahahahahahahahahaaa! The curse worked! You're hideous!!

SNOW. Curse?

ROSE. Hideous?!

> (BELLE *and* ROSE *turn to look at each other slowly.*
> *They both scream.* CINDY *continues to laugh.*)

CINDY. You fools! You thought you could fuck with Cinderella, did you?! Now, I've turned you into a couple of ghouls and they're all gonna laugh at you!! They're all gonna laugh at you!

ROSE. *(Feeling* BELLE*'s fro.)* Actually dear, on second thought, it's not half bad.

BELLE. I was about to say the same thing.

ROSE. Really, do you mean it?

BELLE. Very hip, very mod.

ROSE. *(Suddenly giddy.)* Oh, let's go find a mirror!

BELLE. Come on, I know just where to get one!!

> (*They race offstage.*)

CINDY. WHAT?!

SNOW. Cindy what did you do?! You said that was a magic apple!

CINDY. You imbecile! There's no such thing as magic fruit! Didn't you learn anything from sleepin' in that coffin?!

SNOW. Well, I...

CINDY. It was a curse. A curse meant for each and every one of you!

SNOW. Cindy, how could you? What's the name of this curse?

CINDY. She called it...the curse of Aphrodite.

(ROSE and BELLE come back on, holding the MAGIC MIRROR. They are both gazing into it, fluffing at their new hair, both quite pleased with themselves.)

BELLE. Ohh, Rose, it's très chic!!

ROSE. I absolutely adore it! It's the pièce de résistance!

CINDY. What are you two talking about?! It's the curse of Aphrodite!

BELLE. Oh it's no curse, honey, and I afro-likey!!

ROSE. Belle, we've got the most fabulous locks in the kingdom!

BELLE. We'll be such a hit with all the glitterati!

CINDY. I don't understand!!

BELLE. Here, Snow, have a bite. You've had that same bouffant since you were keepin' house with them dwarves!

SNOW. I'd...rather not.

ROSE. Belle, do you think Charming will like it?

BELLE. Sister, you look like a wild woman. He'll love it. You think he kept you flat on your back before? Just wait!

ROSE. Ohh, thank you Cindy. You've given me such a perfect bridal gift.

CINDY. But I –! But you –! But she –!

(There is a loud crack of thunder, and the lights flicker violently. The front door flies open, and there stands the QUEEN.)

BELLE. And just who the hell are you?

QUEEN. I'm sure Snow White might remember me.

SNOW. Stepmother! But I thought you were dead!

QUEEN. That's what they'd have you believe. It sounds good in the fairy books. But this bulbous sponge that used to be Cinderella knows exactly where I've been, isn't that so?

CINDY. Oh, I know where you've been all right, but if you're coming to collect that mirror, you can forget it. The deal's off!

QUEEN. Why I'm not coming to collect any mirror, my dear. I'm coming to collect you.

CINDY. Me?!

QUEEN. I believe I warned you what would happen if you did not return my property in two days' time.

CINDY. That was in exchange for a curse you old bitch, not a pair of princesses with jheri curl!

QUEEN. What can I say? I never claimed to be the sorcerer's apprentice!

CINDY. Well you better just row your wrinkly ass back to Evil Island, 'cause your curse is a dud!

QUEEN. But of course. Except that you'll be doing the rowing.

CINDY. Come again?

(*The* QUEEN *slaps a chain onto her wrist.*)

QUEEN. With this enchanted chain, you are bound to follow where I lead, and for your blatant disregard of my payment, I hereby sentence you to a life on Evil Island!

CINDY. Get this thing offa me!

QUEEN. Not only that, you shall serve out your years in the house of your stepmother and two stepsisters.

CINDY. Oh my God! Rose, do something! Belle! Snow, you gotta help me!

SNOW. Look at the bright side, Cindy. Just think of all the weight you'll lose.

CINDY. Jesus Christ!

QUEEN. Let's be on our way, Cinderella. That ocean is getting choppy.

SNOW. Stepmother… A moment, if I may?

QUEEN. I really must be going and I do not associate with petty thieves.

SNOW. Well, that's just the thing. You see, I know we didn't have the best relationship when I was growing up…what with you enslaving me, keeping me in rags, casting me out into the woods and then trying to eat my heart… but that was no excuse for me to steal. Stepmother. I believe this belongs to you.

> *(She grabs the mirror from* **BELLE** *and* **ROSE** *and hands it to her. The* **QUEEN** *gives a shudder of ecstasy.)*

QUEEN. Ohhh Gustavo! You're coming home at last.

SNOW. Gustavo??

QUEEN. Poor dear. He must be sound asleep, exhausted from looking at your face all day.

SNOW. Well I hope you can wake him up.

QUEEN. That won't be a problem. I plan to ride him side-saddle, all the way home.

SNOW. I see.

QUEEN. Cinderella! To the rowboat!

CINDY. I'll get you for this! I'll get all of you for this if it's the last thing I –!

> *(Slam.* **CINDY** *and the* **QUEEN** *exit. The sound of shattering glass just offstage. Another pair of shoes bites the dust.)*

(Offstage.) Dammit!

BELLE. Well, that's it for Cindy. I hope the supermarket don't go outa business.

> *(***CHARMING** *enters with two suitcases.)*

CHARMING. *(As he enters.)* Hey Rose. You ready to blow this popsicle stand?

ROSE. I'm ready to blow something, all right.

CHARMING. Rose, my God, what happened to you?!

ROSE. Do you like it?

CHARMING. Do I like it? I never seen somethin' so exotic! And Belle too? A man could go crazy for a coupla chickies like you!

BELLE. What did I tell you?

CHARMING. Hey there, Belle. Ya sure ya don't want to join us in the new digs? I'm still gonna need a goumada!

BELLE. Well, I don't know –

SNOW. Oh, Belle, perhaps you should consider it.

BELLE. And leave you here alone?

SNOW. I'm sure I'll be just fine... And you and Rose complement each other so with your new hair.

CHARMING. One on each arm... We'll be the poshest thing in town!

BELLE. Well, I suppose it's up to Rose. As you know, we've had our differences.

ROSE. I can put the daggers down if you can, darling. I say let's go for it. We'll become fashionistas and take over the entire kingdom.

BELLE. Then I accept! I've always wanted to take over a kingdom!

CHARMING. Well, off we go, then! Snow, baby, it's been swell.

(BELLE *wraps her arms around* SNOW.)

BELLE. Thanks for everything, honey. I'll send for my things in a few days.

ROSE. Yes, darling I can't thank you enough for my royal ball. That gruel ain't so bad after all, and this spider dress held up quite nicely, aside from the fact that it's made me so very sticky.

CHARMING. Not as sticky as you're gonna be later on, baby.

(*They all head for the door.*)

SNOW. I'm so glad for you all. Well goodbye, everyone. I'm sure I'll see you again when you're taking over the kingdom.

(BELLE, CHARMING, *and* ROSE *exit.* SNOW
stands alone for a moment, and then runs quickly
offstage. She runs back on with a small suitcase,
and heads for the door. ALICE *enters from behind*
her.)

ALICE. Going on a little trip?

(SNOW *lets out a small cry of surprise and turns*
to face her.)

SNOW. Oh, Alice for the love of God you have to stop
stalking around!

ALICE. Seems like someone's trying to flee, as it were.

SNOW. As a matter of fact, I do have an engagement to
attend.

ALICE. But I've not yet received my payment and I am
going to tell.

SNOW. Really, Alice. Who are you going to tell? Everyone's
gone! Belle's gone to live with Charming and Rose in
their new palace. Perhaps the Cheshire Cat would like
to hear your tale, but you can no longer blackmail me
with anything!

ALICE. How unfortunate. I simply adore blackmail.

SNOW. But...um... Alice. I do have a payment I could offer
you if you like.

ALICE. Yes?

SNOW. Well, it's just that... Aren't you tired of living in that
rabbit hole?

ALICE. It is rather drafty down there.

SNOW. Well, I'm going away, you see...for a long, long
time. Possibly forever. And I won't be needing this
castle any longer.

ALICE. I see.

SNOW. I know it's not the most fashionable chateau in
town, but I'd hate for it to fall into disrepair. Oh Alice,
would you like it?

ALICE. To have? Your castle? To have it?

SNOW. Yes, to have it, Alice. There are hundreds of rooms. You and your little wonderland friends could run around here like the lunatics that you are from morning till night.

ALICE. What a delightful idea. I accept!

SNOW. Oh good! I'm sure you'll be very happy here, Alice.

ALICE. I'll be happy when you get the hell out of my house! But first I'll go clear those freeloaders out of the ballroom!

> (ALICE *blows her a kiss and exits, just as the doorbell rings.* SNOW *opens it. There stands* BRUCE.)

SNOW. Ohh, Bruce. You came back!

BRUCE. I told you I would, baby, but what's the matter?

SNOW. It's been a terribly trying afternoon is all. So much has happened. I'm so confused.

BRUCE. Maybe this will ease your confusion.

> (*He gives her a big, swooning kiss.*)

SNOW. Well, that definitely helped, I must say.

BRUCE. It's our second chance baby, and second chances don't come knockin' every day.

SNOW. Do you think you could ever love…abandoned goods?

BRUCE. Could I ever, and you already said that you could love a beast.

SNOW. Oh Bruce, I could…and I do.

BRUCE. Well, you know what happens to the girl who loves the beast, don't you?

SNOW. I'm not exactly sure.

BRUCE. Well, she lives happily ever after, of course…

> (*He dips her, kisses her, and picks her up in his arms.*)

…At least for a few months.

(Before she can object, he carries her out the castle door, clocking her head on the door frame on their way out.)

(Blackout.)

The End